THE NECKLACE OF LOVE

Barbara Cartland

Barbara Cartland Ebooks Ltd

This edition © 2020

Copyright Cartland Promotions 1988

ISBNs

9781788672597   EPUB

9781788672603   PAPERBACK

Book design by M-Y Books
m-ybooks.co.uk

THE BARBARA CARTLAND ETERNAL COLLECTION

The Barbara Cartland Eternal Collection is the unique opportunity to collect all five hundred of the timeless beautiful romantic novels written by the world's most celebrated and enduring romantic author.

Named the Eternal Collection because Barbara's inspiring stories of pure love, just the same as love itself, the books will be published on the internet at the rate of four titles per month until all five hundred are available.

The Eternal Collection, classic pure romance available worldwide for all time .

THE LATE DAME BARBARA CARTLAND

Barbara Cartland, who sadly died in May 2000 at the grand age of ninety eight, remains one of the world's most famous romantic novelists. With worldwide sales of over one billion, her outstanding 723 books have been translated into thirty six different languages, to be enjoyed by readers of romance globally.

Writing her first book 'Jigsaw' at the age of 21, Barbara became an immediate bestseller. Building upon this initial success, she wrote continuously throughout her life, producing bestsellers for an astonishing 76 years. In addition to Barbara Cartland's legion of fans in the UK and across Europe, her books have always been immensely popular in the USA. In 1976 she achieved the unprecedented feat of having books at numbers 1 & 2 in the prestigious B. Dalton Bookseller bestsellers list.

Although she is often referred to as the 'Queen of Romance', Barbara Cartland also wrote several historical biographies, six autobiographies and numerous theatrical plays as well as books on life, love, health and cookery. Becoming one of Britain's most popular media personalities and dressed in her trademark pink, Barbara spoke on radio and television about social and political issues, as well as making many public appearances.

In 1991 she became a Dame of the Order of the British Empire for her contribution to literature and her work for humanitarian and charitable causes.

Known for her glamour, style, and vitality Barbara Cartland became a legend in her own lifetime. Best remembered for her wonderful romantic novels and loved by millions of readers worldwide, her books remain treasured for their heroic heroes, plucky heroines and traditional values. But above all, it was Barbara Cartland's overriding belief in the positive power of love to help, heal and improve the quality of life for everyone that made her truly unique.

AUTHOR'S NOTE

I have seen and touched the necklace I have written about in this novel, which is now in the possession of the Countess of Sutherland. This is the true story of what is wrongly called 'The Marie Antoinette Necklace'.

The poor unfortunate Queen of France, who was to be guillotined, never even saw it.

The Comtesse de la Motte, an adventuress descended from a bastard of King Henry II, intrigued to procure the necklace by pretending that it was for Queen Marie Antoinette, but in reality it was for herself.

An enormous and magnificent diamond necklace worth a million and a half *livres*, it had twenty-one huge diamonds in a collet round the neck and four long strands, each containing hundreds of diamonds falling from it and ending in enormous tassels of diamonds.

The Comtesse tricked Prince Louis de Rohan, Cardinal and the Head Chaplain of France, into believing that the Queen wished to acquire it surreptitiously and he agreed to help her.

When a servant arrived to collect the necklace with the forged signature of the Queen, Cardinal Rohan was deceived into believing that it was genuine and handed him the diamond necklace.

The jeweller claimed his money for the necklace and Queen Marie Antoinette disclaimed all knowledge of it. Eventually the truth came out.

The Comtesse de la Motte was sentenced to be flogged and branded on each shoulder with a 'V', *Voleuse*, a thief.

Taking with her the two large diamonds from the collet of the necklace, the Comtesse escaped to London, where she sold the diamonds. She died in 1791.

Cardinal Rohan was acquitted of the charge of fraud, but was deprived of his offices and banished.

This saga gravely discredited and weakened the French Monarchy and was particularly responsible from the beginning for the violence of the French Revolution.

CHAPTER ONE
1839

Kezia, looking out of the window, saw a smart phaeton coming down the drive and gave a cry of delight.

She ran along the passage and down the beautifully carved oak staircase into the hall.

She flung open the door just as her brother pulled his horses to a standstill.

"Perry!" she exclaimed. "I was not expecting you. How exciting!"

Sir Peregrine Falcon handed his reins to a groom and stepped down from the phaeton.

As he reached the steps leading up to the front door, his sister ran down them and flung her arms round his neck.

"It's so wonderful you are back!" she exclaimed.

"You are ruining my cravat," her brother protested, but he was smiling.

They walked arm in arm into the hall together.

"But why have you come home?" she asked. "What has happened? You said you would not be returning for weeks."

"I have some news that I think will please you," Perry replied, "but first I would like something to drink."

Kezia hesitated.

"I am afraid there is only some claret, which I was keeping for your return, or a bottle of cider."

"Cider will do me very well," Perry replied, "and we will most certainly need to keep the claret."

She looked at him in surprise, but he did not explain and she ran to the kitchen quarters.

Humber, the old butler who had served her father faithfully for more than forty years before he died, was sitting in the pantry.

He was polishing the silver and his leg, which was stiff with arthritis, was propped up on a stool.

"Sir Peregrine is back!" Kezia called out excitedly. "And he wants a glass of cider. Don't move, just tell me where the bottle is."

"It's just at the top of the cellar, Miss Kezia, where it keeps nice and cool," Humber replied.

He did not attempt to move to fetch it himself.

If his Master had returned home, it meant he would have to wait at dinner and he could move only with difficulty.

Kezia ran to the cellar door, opened it and found, as Humber had told her, that there were several bottles of homemade cider brewed by one of the more enterprising farmers on the estate.

She took the nearest bottle and carried it down, knowing that her brother would have gone into the library, which was the room that they used when they were alone.

It had at one time been very impressive, but now the curtains were faded, the chairs needed repairing and the carpet was threadbare in several places.

Because her father had always kept a grog tray in a corner of the library with drink on it for anyone who needed it, Peregrine, when he had come into the Baronetcy, had continued the habit.

Now there were no decanters or bottles on the grog tray, only two or three glasses, so that there was plenty of room for Kezia to put the bottle of cider down on the tray.

Her brother then pulled out the cork.

"The roads were incredibly dusty today," he related, "but I managed the journey in three hours, which I consider to be close to a record!"

"Is that counting your stop for luncheon," Kezia asked, "or are you hungry?"

She looked at him anxiously, thinking that there was little in the house and Humber's wife, Betsy, who did the cooking, would be resting.

"No, I had something to eat," Perry replied, "and I deducted that from the time I left London until I reached here. To be truthful in exactly three hours, sixteen minutes and a few seconds."

Kezia laughed.

"No wonder you feel proud."

"I have something more important to be proud of," Perry said.

Kezia looked at him questioningly, wondering what had happened and feeling a little apprehensive.

Life had been so difficult lately.

They were so hard up that she was always afraid that her brother, whom she loved very dearly, would marry for wealth rather than because he was in love.

Although he was an impoverished Baronet, it would not be difficult considering how handsome he was.

He was very much in demand simply because he was charming, good mannered and contributed considerably to the gaiety of every party he attended.

He was indeed an outstanding rider, so that men liked him, while the women became infatuated with him.

Even so Kezia appreciated how humiliating it must be for him that his friends were all richer than he was.

While he accepted a great deal of hospitality, it was completely impossible for him to return it.

In the past some of his closest friends had come to stay, but he could not provide them with beautiful women to entertain them nor the horses they would ride when their host had large stables.

Kezia was therefore alone week after week and month after month in the attractive but dilapidated black and white house that had been in the Falcon family for several generations.

It had been there since the Falcons had moved from Cornwall where the family had started, because Surrey was much closer to London.

They had found Surrey more amusing than living, as Kezia's father had once said, 'at the very end of the world'.

Nevertheless Kezia had always felt that, as her name was Cornish, she really belonged there.

As she waited for her brother to explain why he had come home so unexpectedly, she looked very lovely.

Her gown, which she had made herself, had been washed until it had lost a great deal of its colour and, because she had worn it for several years, it had also become too tight over her curved breasts.

But that did not detract in any way from the gold in her hair with its red tints that caught the sunshine streaming in through the library windows.

Her eyes, which were green, seemed also to catch the sunlight as she waited to hear what Perry had to tell her.

He drank half a glass of the cider before he declared,

"Now hold your breath! I think I have sold the necklace!"

Kezia gave a little gasp and then she cried,

"Are you really sure? Are you going to get what you have beeb asking for it?"

"I am practically certain that, when the Marquis sees it, he will not only buy it but pay exactly the sum I want."

"The Marquis?" Kezia questioned.

Perry took another sip of cider before he responded,

"The Marquis de Bayeux."

"French," Kezia murmured.

"Norman," her brother corrected her.

"But how do you know him and how did you manage to tell him about the necklace?"

"I first met the Marquis over a year ago when he was buying horses at Tattersalls," Perry explained. "I have seen him on and off at Race Meetings, as he often visits England. Then two days ago, one of my friends, Harry Perceval – you remember Harry?"

"Yes, of course," Kezia answered.

"Well, Harry brought him to White's Club and, as he entered, I heard somebody behind me say, 'I saw Bayeux in Bond Street today buying diamonds for a beautiful creature, who was already weighted down with them'!"

Perry paused.

"It was then it struck me that he might be just the person we were looking for."

Kezia clasped her hands together.

"Oh, Perry, I do hope you are right. We need the money so desperately and, as you have said so often, it would be foolish for us to accept the ridiculously small sum that the jewellers have already offered us."

"If the Marquis comes up to scratch," Perry said, "it will certainly have been worthwhile waiting for the right man to come along even though it has been extremely uncomfortable at times."

He looked round the room, taking in at a glance how shabby everything was.

Then he turned to look at his sister.

"It is you who has suffered the worst," he said frankly, "and I swear, Kezia, I will make it up to you. You shall come to London, have pretty gowns and we will arrange for one of our relations to present you to Queen Victoria at Buckingham Palace."

"It sounds wonderful!" Kezia replied. "At the same time I think I would rather have a decent horse to ride than a grand gown to dance in!"

"You shall have both," Perry answered. "But now, as the Marquis is arriving in two days' time, you have to disappear."

Kezia looked at her brother in astonishment.

"What do you mean – disappear?"

"What I say," Perry replied.

"But – I don't – understand."

"Well, Monsieur le Marquis is not only a very wealthy man and owns a great deal of property in Normandy and I believe that his Château is magnificent. But he also has a house in Paris, which is as notorious as he is himself!"

"He is notorious for what?" Kezia asked.

Perry hesitated for a moment.

Then he said,

"For running after women. He has broken more hearts than Casanova and is such a Don Juan that no woman is safe with him!"

"So that is why you will not let me see him."

"Exactly," Perry answered her. "You are too young, too innocent and much too pretty!"

Kezia laughed.

"How can you be so ridiculous? If the Marquis has, as you say, pursued lovely women in France, he is not likely to look at me."

"I see your point," Perry admitted, "But he *is* dangerous."

"Forewarned is forearmed," Kezia pointed out.

"It is not only what the Marquis will do," Perry said, "but Harry was telling me that he possesses some strange charisma about him that makes women throw themselves at his feet. According to Harry he has only to look at them and they behave like lunatics!"

Kezia laughed again.

"I don't believe a word of it. Even if the Marquis did look at me, which is very unlikely, he sounds the sort of man who would frighten me. So I would be too busy running away from him to do anything so foolish as to fall in love with him!"

"You cannot be certain of that," Perry replied, "so you must understand that you must go away for the two days he is here."

"And who is going to look after him?" Kezia asked.

"It is not only him."

"He is bringing someone else?"

"He is and I call it impertinent and almost an insult, but I can hardly object."

"What are you saying?" Kezia asked her, feeling rather confused at the sudden turn of events.

"The Marquis left a note for me at White's Club to say that he would be arriving here on Thursday and bringing with him a certain Madame de Salres."

"Who is she?"

"She is his current – "

Here Perry stopped, realising that what he had been just about to say would have been indiscreet.

After a poignant pause he went on,

"I understand that she is a – very close friend."

"What you are saying is that she is in love with him," Kezia said. "Well, that makes it quite clear that he will not notice me and I am sure, if the Marquis is interested enough to bring a lady friend with him, he is definitely enamoured of her."

"That is very likely true," Perry agreed reluctantly. "At the same time he has no right to bring her into the house when you are present."

"But, you have said, I will not be here," Kezia remarked logically. "You obviously did not tell him I would be acting as hostess."

Perry put down his empty glass.

"There is no use in arguing about it," he said firmly. "You must stay away. Perhaps you could stay with some friends or with the Vicar in the village."

"Surely the Vicar would think it very strange if I ask him if I can stay with him because you are entertaining a man who you don't approve of?" Kezia said. "And you know that we cannot say that we are selling the necklace or it might be picked up by the newspapers."

Perry frowned.

"Oh, stop making difficulties, there must be somewhere you can go!"

"And what do you think will happen if I do?" Kezia asked. "You know who we have in the house, old Humber, whose rheumatics are so bad he can only just shuffle into the dining room."

She paused to catch his breath and then went on,

"While Betsy is a good cook, she cannot manage anything complicated and certainly not a dish that would be palatable to a Frenchman."

Perry was listening with a frown between his eyes, but he did not interrupt as Kezia went on,

"You know that Mrs. Jones comes in from the village for two hours every day, but she could not manage the beds without me and she forgets what she is supposed to do unless I remind her constantly."

Kezia paused and Perry said irritably,

"Well, try to find somebody else."

"And train them in two days? You know that is impossible!"

"Nothing is impossible," Perry parried crossly, "and, if we lose the Marquis, we may never find another buyer for the necklace."

"Why can he not view it in London?" Kezia asked.

"Because when I told him that it had been in our possession ever since the 1789 French Revolution, I happened to mention that my grandfather had bought it for my grandmother to wear when she was painted by the Master artist, Reynolds.

"'Then it is a painting I must see!' the Marquis exclaimed. "I have several Reynolds in my collection and consider him one of the best English artists there has ever been, especially when it came to painting women."

"'I agree with you,' I said and it was then that he asked himself to stay with us."

"I do see that you could hardly take the picture to London when it is so large," Kezia nodded.

"What was I to do," Perry asked, "except agree that he come here, but I had no idea that he was going to bring some fastidious Frenchwoman with him."

Kezia gave a little cry.

"If she is fastidious and therefore uncomfortable, she may persuade him to leave earlier than he intends and so not buy the necklace."

Perry saw the point of what his sister was saying and he walked across the room to the window.

He looked out at the garden, which had grown very wild and unruly with no one to tend it.

"I have been planning all the way down here," he said, as if he spoke to himself, "the improvements that we can make to the house. To start with we have to mend the roof and put new panes of glass in the windows."

"We need a new stove in the kitchen," Kezia said. "It is a miracle that the old one has lasted as long as it has and, if you don't do something about the pump, we shall have no water unless we fetch it from the lake."

"I know, I know," Perry groaned. "That is why we have to make sure that the Marquis is satisfied not only with the necklace but also with the house and the food he eats as well."

"Therefore," Kezia asserted positively, "you cannot possibly do without me!"

Perry put his hand up to his forehead.

"I am trying to look after you," he said. "I am trying to make sure that you don't make a fool of yourself over a man who will go back to France and forget you even exist."

Kezia threw up her hands.

"What can I say to convince you that I will not fall in love with him? All I will do is to make him so comfortable and feed him so well that he will be in a good humour and then pay up!"

Perry walked back to stand in front of the fireplace.

He was gazing at his sister as if he had never seen her before and he then commented,

"You know, if you were decently dressed and your hair was arranged in a fashionable style, you would be a sensation in London!"

"Thank you, dearest," Kezia said. "It is very nice of you to talk like that, but you know as well as I do that unless we sell the necklace, I will never go to London and the only people who are likely to think me a sensation here are Humber, Betsy, the rooks and the rabbits!"

Perry laughed.

"That is true enough anyway. But I have the uncomfortable feeling that if I let you stay, however reasonable it sounds, it is something I shall bitterly regret later!"

Because he sounded so anxious, Kezia rose from the sofa where she had been sitting and went to his side.

She kissed his cheek before she said,

"You are a wonderful brother and you have always been very kind to me, but now you have to trust me."

"I trust you," Perry assured her. "It's that damned Frenchman I don't trust any further than I could throw him!"

There was silence between them and he then realised that his sister was looking shocked because he had sworn.

"I am so sorry," he said. "I only wish to God that Mama were here. She would know how to cope with him."

"Of course she would," Kezia murmured softly.

Then she gave a sudden cry.

"I have an idea!"

Perry walked again to the window and then turned his head back to ask her,

"What is it?"

"It is actually what you said just now about Mama being here. If Mama and Papa were entertaining the Marquis and the fastidious Frenchwoman who he is bringing with him, there would be no difficulty."

"Of course not," he agreed, "except that I think Mama would have been rather shocked that they were travelling together without a chaperone."

He thought to himself, although he did not say it out loud, that it was *damned* insulting of the Frenchman to bring his mistress into a respectable household.

But it was something that he could not say to Kezia.

"My idea," Kezia was saying slowly, "is that I should be your wife!"

There was silence while her brother stared at her.

"What are you saying?"

"You think that the Marquis would make advances to me because I am an unattached woman, but he would not dare approach me if I was his hostess and your wife!"

It shot through Perry's mind that the fact that Kezia was married would not inhibit the Marquis as she thought it would.

Madame de Salres doubtless had a husband, who had been left behind in Paris.

Equally he could see that it would certainly make things better if Kezia was a 'married woman,' provided that they had not been married for long.

Kezia was waiting for his response and Perry thought over very carefully what she had said before he replied cautiously,

"It is a possibility."

"It is a sensible solution," Kezia corrected him. "I can stay here and look after him. I can make sure what servants we do have will carry out their duties and I assure you I shall be too busy doing all that besides coping with most of the cooking to philander with the Marquis, however attractive he may be!"

"I shall certainly be a very jealous husband!" Perry remarked with a smile on his lips.

Kezia clapped her hands together.

"Of course you will and he could hardly be so thick-skinned as to flirt with me in front of you."

Perry did not reply and she went on,

"Besides, if he is busy with Madame de Salres, why should he take any notice of me?"

Perry wondered why he had not thought of this himself.

At the same time he was suddenly aware that his sister seemed even more beautiful than she had when he had last been at home.

The Falcon women were famous for their beauty all down the centuries and there was plenty of evidence of it in the portraits of them that hung on the walls of the house.

As he remembered this, he gave an exclamation and said,

"The idea is hopeless!"

"Why?" Kezia asked.

"Because you are very like the portrait of Mama that hangs in the drawing room and Papa always said that you resemble the wife of the fourth Baronet, who was acclaimed as a great beauty by all the Officers who fought with the Duke of Marlborough in France!"

Kezia thought for a moment and next she suggested,

"Then I am a cousin and I was also a Falcon and we fell in love because we have known each other since we were children."

"I suppose that might be a good explanation," Perry said doubtfully.

"It is a sensible one if you think about it and, if the Marquis is interested in the house, I shall have to know all about the Falcons."

She paused to smile at him before continuing,

"It is reasonable therefore to explain that, as a Falcon myself, I was brought up on the history of the family, their ghosts and, of course, 'the Bad Baronet', who is responsible for our present predicament."

Perry did not speak and after a moment Kezia carried on,

"As I have told you before, I shall be very delighted if we can sell the necklace. I have always believed it to be unlucky."

"It is going to be extremely lucky for us if the Marquis pays the money I am asking for it."

Kezia was not listening to him.

She was thinking of how the diamond necklace that her grandfather had bought for his wife had caused one of the greatest scandals of the eighteenth century.

It was in 1785 that the Comtesse de la Motte, an avowed adventuress, had seen the most expensive and fantastic necklace that had ever been made in Paris.

She had then persuaded the Cardinal de Rohan to help her convince the jeweller that the necklace was to be given to Queen Marie Antoinette.

Instead the Comtesse had stolen it and her subsequent trial had electrified the whole of France.

The Comtesse was arrested, but she then escaped from prison and fled to London. And she took with her twenty-one diamonds that she had removed from the necklace.

They were only a small part of what had been the most enormous and magnificent piece of jewellery of the era, besides being the most expensive.

The diamonds were arranged in a new setting and were very beautiful when they were presented to then Lady Falcon, the grandmother of Perry and Kezia.

Because they had caused such a commotion and so much suffering in their wake, many historians at the time averred that the scandal had been directly responsible for the outbreak of the French Revolution.

Kezia, therefore, had always considered them to be unlucky.

They were locked away in a safe place that would have been difficult for a burglar to locate and Kezia had never put them round her neck.

She did not like to remember that her mother had worn them at a hunt ball three months before she died.

It was largely because the necklace was so valuable that it had been difficult to sell and Perry had been determined after it had been valued that he would obtain the right price for it or it would remain where it was.

"It is the one saleable *objet d'art* we possess," he had said to his sister, "and the only hope we ever have of putting this house back in shape and being able to enjoy ourselves as we should."

Kezia agreed with him, but was aware that she longed to be able to employ younger and more active servants.

It broke her heart to see the house growing more and more dilapidated month after month. She loved her home and she loved too the old people in the village who were really their responsibility, but they could do so little for them.

Now, she thought, although there was very little time, she must make the Marquis and the Frenchwoman with him happy and comfortable.

Otherwise she was quite certain that they would leave as quickly as possible without taking the necklace with them.

She felt as if her head was whirling with the thought of all that she had to do, but aloud she said,

"Do stop wasting time in arguing, Perry! I will be 'Lady Falcon' for the two days that the Marquis is staying here and I promise I will be so enraptured with my 'handsome husband', I will not have time even to look at Satan if he was tempting me with an apple!"

"It is exactly what he may be doing," Perry replied. "And you can understand, however tempting the apple may be, you are to refuse to accept it!"

"I will do exactly as you tell me," Kezia acknowledged, "and now we have to get busy."

Perry looked at her questioningly and she ticked off with her fingers,

"We need champagne, young lamb from the farmer, chickens, ducks and fish."

She smiled before she added,

"There are plenty of trout in the stream if you can catch them!"

"The only thing I thought of was the champagne," Perry said. "And that is why I left the phaeton outside so that I could drive into Guildford at once."

"There are dozens of things I want too, but your horses will be tired, so I will make a list of them for tomorrow."

Perry walked towards the door.

"I can only hope," he pointed out, "that this deal comes off, otherwise I shall not be able to pay for the champagne or anything else I buy!"

Kezia gave an exclamation of horror.

"Do you mean you are 'below hatches'? Oh, Perry, you have not been gambling again?"

"I was told it was a certainty," he admitted bitterly, leaving the library and slamming the door behind him.

Kezia put her hand up to her head.

She knew what lay in front of her was going to be a gigantic task. It meant that, besides getting the house ready, she would have to cook a large number of the more complicated dishes that Betsy would be incapable of managing.

It was a blessing that it was early summer and therefore not every course would have to be hot.

But, if Betsy grew tired, there would be too many things to be done at the same time.

She also had to impress upon Betsy and Humber that they were not to address her as 'Miss Kezia' as was usual, but as 'my Lady'.

'And all this,' she said beneath her breath, 'for a Frenchman who will not appreciate any of it, but take it all as a matter of course.'

Also he and his fastidious friend would doubtless disparage the way she was dressed and look down their noses at the house.

For a moment she felt humiliated and then she put up her chin defiantly.

She was a Falcon and however rich the Marquis might be, her blood was as good if not better than his.

He might be, for all she knew, a descendant of William the Conqueror, but the Falcons were living in Cornwall before he invaded England in the year 1066.

The history books told that there were Falcons who fought with King Harold at the Battle of Hastings.

'If the Marquis thinks that he can trample on Perry and me, he is going to be mistaken,' she muttered to herself. 'And I will make it quite clear when he arrives that we speak to him as equals.'

Then, as she began to walk to the door, she saw a reflection of herself in the one gilt mirror hanging on the wall.

It showed her just how unfashionable and worn her gown was and she recognised very clearly how, if the

Marquis did not disparage her appearance, any woman, and especially a French one, would be contemptuous of her to say the least of it.

'I have to find something decent to wear,' Kezia told herself firmly.

She knew that she should be going into the kitchen to prepare Betsy for what lay ahead.

Instead she ran up the stairs and into the room that led off the main bedroom where her mother had always slept.

It had originally been a powder room, but then quite a large one and Lady Falcon had, however, converted it into a room where she kept all her clothes.

"I have always thought it to be unnecessary and very unromantic," she had said, "to keep one's clothes in a bedroom unless it is absolutely necessary."

She had therefore made it so beautiful that it was more like a sitting room.

"Wardrobes are ugly pieces of furniture," she had insisted.

So they were banished to the powder room, which had not been used since the end of the previous century.

Because, after her mother had died, Kezia had kept her room almost sacred, nobody had stayed in it and she seldom bothered to enter the powder room, where her mother's clothes still remained.

Once or twice when she had either grown out of her own clothes or they had fallen to bits, she had thought she would find something that had belonged to her.

For the last two years, however, there had been no necessity for her to look anything but what she called a 'beggar maid' in her own garments.

When Perry came home he came alone and, after the period of mourning was over, the neighbours seemed to have forgotten that she was there and seldom sent her invitations for any event.

There was no money for horses so she could not hunt in the winter.

The old horses that carried her to the farms when she called on the tenants or went down to the village were reliable, but they were so slow that she usually preferred to walk rather than ride.

Now, as she entered her mother's wardrobe room, there was the fragrance of the white violet perfume that Lady Falcon had always distilled every spring.

There was also the scent of lavender in the little muslin bags that she had made and put in the linen cupboard and amongst her undergarments.

For a moment the perfume brought back her mother so vividly that Kezia felt the tears come into her eyes.

Then she told herself severely that there was no time for sentimentality.

She just had to look to see if there was anything that she could wear to entertain the Marquis in.

If, as she suspected, her mother's gowns would make her look older and so were not appropriate for a very young girl, that was exactly what she wanted.

She opened the doors of the wardrobe and for a moment the kaleidoscope of soft colours seemed to blind her eyes.

Then, as impatiently she brushed away the tears, she saw that there were several gowns that she could play the part of Perry's wife in.

Her mother's dressing table stood beside the window and she sat down for a moment on the stool to look at herself in the mirror.

Then she did not see her own face, but her mother's and she prayed in her heart,

'Help me, Mama – and help us to sell the necklace, which will give Perry so many things he wants and restore the house to the way it ought to look – instead of the state it is in now.'

Kezia had the strange feeling that it was her mother who smiled back at her rather than her own reflection.

Then she jumped to her feet, closed the doors of the wardrobe and, opening the door, ran as quickly as she could along the passage and down the stairs.

There was so much to do and she really must not waste a moment.

She knew that it was only by a superhuman effort of hers that she would be ready for the notorious Marquis when he arrived.

'And when he does,' Kezia told herself, 'I shall be so exhausted by everything that has to be done that if he is, as Perry says, a modern Casanova, there will be nothing he can do or say that will get the slightest response from me!'

She was laughing at her own joke as she then pushed open the baize door, which needed recovering and which led into the kitchen quarters.

Old Humber was by himself in the pantry cleaning the few silver dishes that she and Perry used when they were alone.

Kezia wondered frantically if he would ever have time to clean the candelabra that were to be put on the table at dinner.

There were also *entrée* dishes, the coffee pot, sugar bowl and cream jug, besides the salvers that were used whenever they had guests staying in the house.

'The whole thing is impossible!' she told herself despondently.

Then once again her pride told her that there was no such word and what had to be done must be done and the sooner the better.

Old Humber, still with his leg on a stool, looked up and waited for her to speak.

The sunshine coming through the window showed up what was left of his white hair and the lines on his face and the gnarled fingers of his hand that held the teapot were swollen with rheumatism.

In a voice that sounded even to herself weak and inaudible, Kezia said,

"I-I have something to – tell you, Humber – and it is very important!"

CHAPTER TWO

Kezia hurried into the breakfast room to find Perry eating his breakfast.

"I am sorry to be late," she began breathlessly, "but there has been such a lot to do."

She had been out of her bed since six o'clock tidying the drawing room and she had also put finishing touches to the bedrooms that would be occupied by the Marquis de Bayeux and Madame de Salres.

She had been rather surprised when Perry had said to her,

"Put our guests next door to each other."

Kezia had raised her eyes.

"Next door?" she asked. "I thought Madame de Salres would appreciate the Rose Room, which, after Mama's, is, I always think, the most beautiful room in the whole house."

It was her mother who had Christened the rooms with the names of flowers.

She had tried where possible to have the colours of them in the curtains, the cushions and, because they had a large collection, the pictures.

"That would be a mistake," Perry insisted. "If you put the Marquis in the Water Lily Room, which overlooks the garden, then Madame de Salres must be next door."

"I cannot imagine why," Kezia said.

Perry thought how he could offer her a plausible explanation.

Then he said,

"She might feel lonely or afraid in a strange house where there are few people."

"Oh, of course," Kezia agreed. "I never thought of that. Then she will have to go into the Lilac Room, which is very pretty."

"I am sure that would suit her well," Perry replied with relief.

The room, however, had not been used for some time. Although Mrs. Jones had cleaned it rather perfunctorily, Kezia found that there was still so much for her to do to make it as comfortable as she was sure the Frenchwoman would expect.

Now, as she sat down at the table, Perry took up a letter that was lying by his place and looked at it frowning.

"What is – it?" Kezia asked anxiously.

She had a sudden fear that after all their optimism the Marquis had changed his mind and was not coming to stay.

There was a pause before Perry answered,

"This is a letter from the Marquis's secretary, who informs me that he will be arriving at about five o'clock."

"That is a sensible hour," Kezia said with relief. "As he is French, he will not expect tea and, after you have given them both something to drink, Madame, at any rate, can rest before dinner."

"I thought that was what you would think," her brother replied, "but the secretary also says that the Marquis will be arriving with a groom and another carriage will bring down the luggage with his valet and Madame's lady's maid."

Kezia gave a little gasp as her brother went on,

"There will be two outriders as well!"

"I just don't believe it!" Kezia cried. "How can two people require five servants with them?"

"I warned you that the Marquis considers himself of the greatest importance and he is rich enough to afford five hundred attendants if he needs them!"

"But – how can we possibly – accommodate all those people?" Kezia asked helplessly.

"We cannot," Perry said firmly. "The outriders and the groom must stay at *The Fox and Hounds* in the village."

"They will be very uncomfortable there," Kezia murmured.

"We shall have to accommodate the lady's maid and the valet," Perry went on as if she had not spoken, "and I admit that I should have thought of this before."

"I suppose I should have too, but it is so long since Mama could afford a lady's maid and you have never had a valet, so I just forgot."

"So did I to be honest," Perry said, "but then we will have to accommodate them in the house."

"There are plenty of bedrooms, as you well know, but it means cleaning them all out and making the beds and I have so many other things to do."

"Surely Betsy can help you?" Perry suggested.

"Betsy is already collapsing," Kezia answered, "and, although Jenny, the girl I have from the village, is doing her best, she has not the slightest idea of what she is expected to do and is often more trouble than she is worth!"

Perry looked at the letter again and then slipped it into the pocket of his coat.

"Why ever was I such a fool as to let the Marquis persuade me to invite him here?" he mumbled.

"You must not blame yourself," Kezia said quickly. "We will manage somehow. But, if servants are uncomfortable, they always grumble and that may upset the Marquis."

Perry did not answer, he only rose from his chair and said,

"I am now going to inspect the stables to see if they are decent enough for his horses. I expected two and now he is bringing four."

"Perhaps you will have the chance of riding one of them," Kezia proposed.

But she did not think that her brother had heard her, for he had already left the breakfast room.

She rose from the table and, picking up the plates and cups, stacked them onto a tray and carried them into the kitchen.

She told Jenny to wash them up and be very very careful not to break anything.

"I be doin' me best, Miss Kezia," she said.

There was a little pile of broken crockery already on the dresser and Kezia thought with a sigh that, unless the Marquis bought the necklace, they would never be replaced.

She went upstairs to find Mrs. Jones and asked her to clean out the two rooms where the lady's maid and the valet would sleep.

She had intended to put them in the servants' quarters on the second floor, which had always been used in the past, but then she had an idea.

There were two bachelor rooms, which were not nearly as impressive or as elaborate as the State Rooms. They had been used before her father died when he had friends who came only for one night, usually to hunt the next day.

'I will put the Marquis's servants in those rooms,' she then decided, 'and at least the beds are comfortable and the rooms are in fairly good repair.'

When she and Mrs. Jones looked at them, she found, however, that soot had fallen down one chimney and making a considerable mess on the hearthrug. And owing to a crack in one of the windowpanes, starlings had nested in the other.

By the time all this had been cleaned up it was then time for luncheon and Perry was shouting for her up the stairs.

It was a rather sparse meal, but she thought that it was a mistake to ask Betsy to cook anything before dinner tonight.

Everything cold she had already cooked herself and had arranged the dishes carefully so that all old Humber had to do was to bring them into the dining room.

She knew that she could trust Betsy with the leg of lamb. She herself had picked the new peas from the garden and the very smallest of the new potatoes, which, with plenty of butter, would be very palatable.

There was also asparagus, rather thin and wild, which would be served with the main course.

By four o'clock Kezia was feeling as if her legs would no longer carry her and what she wanted to do more than anything else was to lie down.

She had arranged most of the flowers the day before and they made all the difference to the drawing room, which had not been opened for so long.

She had also put a large bowl of carnations in the hall and it made a vivid touch of colour against the darkness of the walls and the carved oak staircase.

Because it was what her mother would have done, she had put water lilies that were just coming into flower in the Marquis's bedroom.

Next, because the white lilac was over, she put a vase of lilies in Madame de Salres's bedroom.

She had also added a bowl of white roses and thought that, against the mauve curtains, they made the room look really lovely.

'I would only hope that she is grateful for all the trouble we have taken,' Kezia said to herself and then laughed.

She was quite certain, coming from Paris or was it the Marquis's Château in Normandy that Madame de Salres would undoubtedly disparage anything quite so simple as an English country home.

Especially, she thought, one that needed an enormous amount of money spent on it to make it look as it had been in the old days.

When she reached her bedroom, she remembered because there had been so much to do that she had not yet decided which of her mother's gowns she would receive the Marquis in.

She had already chosen the one she would wear in the evening, which was of emerald green gauze so that it did not need pressing.

Kezia knew that, if she had to keep the irons on the kitchen stove, it would interfere with the cooking, besides, Betsy grew agitated if there were too many people around her.

Now Kezia opened the wardrobe and, because the gowns reminded her how much she missed her mother, for a moment she had an impulse not to wear any of them.

She could greet the Marquis in one of her own outgrown over-washed gowns.

Then she realised that she would be letting Perry down.

If the Marquis was as formidable as he feared, she should try to charm him into a good temper otherwise the whole visit would be a disaster.

She therefore took from its hanger a gown that she had always loved to see her mother in because it was the blue of forge-me-nots and also the colour of her mother's eyes.

Kezia was undoubtedly like Lady Falcon. But her eyes were a different hue and her hair was a little redder.

Lady Falcon had actually had the colouring that foreigners often described as a 'Perfect English Rose' and Kezia thought it a pity that she was different.

Perhaps, she thought, if the Marquis noticed her at all, he would not admire her.

There was, however, no time to worry and she hurried up to her bedroom and put on the gown, which was slightly out of date.

Skirts had grown much larger in the last two years. The young Queen Victoria had set the fashion for evening gowns that were off-the-shoulder, waists that were tiny and skirts that flared out over what appeared to be a multitude of petticoats.

Lady Falcon's gown was far more restrained after the fashion set by Queen Adelaide, who had always been extremely prim and proper.

Yet because Kezia was so thin, her waist was tiny and, although the skirts should have been larger, the whole gown revealed the grace of her figure.

Also, although she did not realise it, it made her look very young.

She had no time to arrange her hair in a fashionable manner, but just parted it in the centre and secured it at the back of her head.

Then when she was about to examine her reflection in the mirror to see if there was any way that she could improve her appearance, she heard Perry call her from downstairs,

"Kezia! Where are you? They are turning into the drive."

Running as quickly as she could along the passage, Kezia reached the top of the stairs.

Now she could see through one of the many windows in the hall that there were horses crossing the bridge over the lake.

Even at that distance she realised that they were a magnificent team, perfectly matched and jet-black.

The groom driving them wore a top hat on the side of his head.

When they drew nearer, she could see that there was a lady beside him wearing a bonnet on which fluttered a number of feathers.

Then, as she stood there staring, Perry said,

"Hurry up, Kesia, you should be in the drawing room. I will wait to receive them in the hall."

As he spoke, Humber, in his long-tailed coat, came shuffling from under the stairs to the front door.

Kezia had a quick glimpse of two outriders just behind the phaeton and thought that their horses looked unusually fine.

She reached the hall and, running past Perry, hurried into the drawing room.

Her heart was beating loudly and she felt breathless.

It was only because of the speed that she had hurried down the stairs at and, because now that the Marquis was actually arriving, she felt frightened.

So much depended on his visit.

If anything went wrong, she was aware that there would be many more bills to meet than there had been a week ago and she had no idea how they could pay them.

She had found a man in the village who had come up to help Humber and who would carry the luggage upstairs.

He had been in service when he was young, but he had now gone into partnership with the blacksmith.

He did not wish to go back to the days when he was, as he had said, a slave taking orders from anyone who wished to give them to him.

It was only because Kezia's father had always been kind to him when he gave a hand during the hunting season that he now condescended to come to the house for the two nights that the Marquis was staying with them.

"I ain't wearin' no livery, miss!" he had stipulated firmly.

"No, of course not," Kezia said quickly, although she hoped that was what he would do. "If you will just carry the dishes to the dining room door so that Humber can take them in, and look after our guest's valet, I would be very very grateful."

She pleaded with him so prettily that it would have taken a heart of stone to refuse her!

So Douglas, somewhat reluctantly, had agreed to help.

Of course she promised to pay him more than she would have paid somebody completely untrained.

It would be worth it if the 'end justified the means', she mused.

'If the Marquis does not buy the necklace,' Kezia thought in a panic, 'then we shall have to find something else to sell.'

The pictures as well as the furniture was all entailed onto the son that Perry had said he would never be able to afford.

Now, waiting for the Marquis to arrive, Kezia found herself praying that he would buy the necklace and, having made up his mind to do so, would leave as soon as possible.

Then, as she heard voices in the hall, she moved a little nearer to the fireplace, thinking that it would look less contrived than if she stood near the door.

She could hear Perry talking and now, although he sounded at his ease, underneath she knew that he was tense and anxious.

Then there was a deep voice answering him and a moment later the door opened.

It was Madame de Salres who came in first and the moment Kezia saw her she felt her heart sink.

Never had she imagined any woman could look so smart, although she was aware that '*chic*' was probably the right word.

She wore fantastic jewellery in a way that did not make it look vulgar or overpowering.

For a moment Kezia had no eyes for the man who walked behind her.

As Madame de Salres moved almost like a ship in full sail down the drawing room, she advanced a little way to meet her.

"May I present my wife," she heard Perry saying.

As she curtseyed, Madame de Salres held out an exquisitely gloved hand.

"I do hope you have had a good journey," Kezia enquired in her soft voice.

"Well, it was abominable," Madame replied. "The dust in your country is – 'ow do you say – a cloud of darkness and I am enveloped in it!"

She spoke as though it was Kezia's fault.

And then a voice from behind her came in perfect English except for the slightest accent,

"As usual, Yvonne, you exaggerate your suffering, although I too am delighted to arrive at my destination!"

For a moment Kezia could not look at the Marquis even though she thought that his voice sounded attractive.

Then, as she curtseyed, he raised her hand perfunctorily to his lips and, as she lifted her eyes, she found that he was not in the least what she had expected.

She had somehow had a picture in her mind that being French he would be dark, small and perhaps because of what Perry had said about him, somehow like the Devil in the picture books.

Instead he was taller than Perry with broad shoulders and the narrow hips of an athlete.

His hair was most certainly dark, but astonishingly, until she remembered that he came from Normandy, his eyes were blue.

They were not the blue of her mother's, which had been like the blue of a summer sky, but the dark blue of the sea.

For a moment she was so surprised that she could not speak.

Then, as she looked at him, she realised that there was a slightly mocking smile on his lips and it gave him an unexpectedly cynical expression that was out of keeping with the rest of his face.

"It is very kind of you to have us to stay," the Marquis began. "As I expect your husband has told you, I am very eager to see the necklace and also your pictures."

"I do hope that you will not be disappointed," Perry said before Kezia could speak. "I have heard that your own collection is magnificent."

"I like to think so," the Marquis smiled, "but there is always room for improvement, as I am sure that you yourself find."

"Yes, of course," Perry said hastily. "And now, let me offer you some refreshment and I am sure that nothing today would be more suitable than the wine of your own country."

He turned to the side table, where Kezia had put the wine cooler that Humber had sat up half the night polishing.

In it was a bottle of champagne that Perry had bought yesterday.

Perry poured out two glasses and then carried one to Madame de Salres, who had seated herself, rather disdainfully, Kezia thought, on the sofa.

She was spreading out her skirt to accentuate the fullness of it.

"A glass of champagne is somethin' I certainly need!" she said. "My throat is so dry I can 'ardly croak!"

"Then drink quickly," the Marquis said, "so that your dulcet tones, which you have often told me resemble that of a nightingale, can be heard in this attractive house, which I am sure sports a dozen nightingales in the garden."

Kezia laughed.

"We certainly have a few," she admitted, "but many more rooks and crows as is usual in England."

And the Marquis took a sip from his glass.

Then he said,

"Tell me about your home, Lady Falcon. From what I have seen of it already, I find it charming. I imagine that it was built in the reign of King Charles II."

"That is clever of you," Kezia exclaimed. "It was built after the Restoration, when the Falcon of the day was spared being executed in the Tower of London by just a few hours!"

"You must tell me the whole story, the Marquis suggested, "and I know that I shall find it fascinating."

There was just something in the way he spoke that made Kezia realise that in an obscure manner he was paying her a compliment.

She blushed and then, turning to Perry, said,

"Have you explained, dearest, that the coachman and the outriders have to stay at *The Fox and Hounds*?"

She saw as she spoke that Perry had forgotten and he said swiftly,

"No, but I will go and tell them at once while you explain to the Marquis how sorry we are that we cannot accommodate them here."

Kezia drew in her breath.

"I hope – you will – not mind," she said to him apologetically, "but, as we are very short-staffed at present and as our servants are rather old, we could not at such short notice have so many people here – in the house."

"I quite understand," the Marquis replied, "and it is something I should have thought of myself."

"No – no – of course not! Why should you?" Kezia said. "And I am very sure that the landlord of the inn will make them comfortable."

She had in fact called on Mr. Geary, the landlord of *The Fox and Hounds*, when she had gone into the village for provisions.

She had begged him to do what he could for the Marquis's servants.

"You knows we ain't be used to visitors, miss," the old man had replied, "and the Missus don't 'ave much time to keep the rooms as they should be."

"I know it is late to ask you," Kezia had said to him quickly.

"Well, I'll do me best. I'll give 'em a bed, but what do they plan to eat?" Mr. Geary had said. "You knows well as I do they'd be more comfortable up at the 'ouse."

"We just cannot manage to look after any more people," Kezia said, "so please, Mr. Geary, help us. It is very important that they should not be uncomfortable and in consequence – disagreeable."

Mr. Geary had laughed.

"I can't say 'no' to you, miss, 'avin' known you since you were a little 'un, but I can't do more than me best and that's all I can say."

Kezia thought that it was what she might say for herself too.

Now she was afraid that, if the Marquis was annoyed, everything might go wrong.

Hastily and to make everything seem better she said,

"I can promise that your horses will be comfortable."

There was a twist to the Marquis's lips as he said,

"I think, Lady Falcon, that you are offering me a chocolate to take away the taste of the medicine."

Kezia laughed.

"That is what I always had as a child."

"I did too," the Marquis said, "but don't worry, I am sure my staff will be comfortable and, if they are not, they will just have to manage."

As if she thought that she was being neglected, Madame Salres piped up,

"I shall be uncomfortable until I 'ave washed ze dust out of my 'air. Will you show me my room? I would like to rest before dinner."

"Yes, of course," Kezia replied, "and, as we are in the country, we thought you would not mind if we have dinner at seven-thirty."

Madame de Salres held up her hands in horror. "Seven-thirty!" she exclaimed. "In Paris I never dine before nine o'clock."

"You are not in Paris now!" the Marquis retorted. "And, as I will then be hungry, I shall welcome dinner at seven-thirty."

Kezia looked at him gratefully while Madame de Salres with a shrug of her shoulders walked towards the door.

Kezia hurried to follow her, but before she did so she turned and said very quietly to the Marquis so that only he could hear,

"Thank – you!"

She spoke quite naturally, the way that she would have spoken to anyone who had eased the cares of the household.

She did not see the surprise in his blue eyes.

As Kezia took Madame de Salres into the Lilac Room, she thought it would be difficult, fastidious though she might be, for her to find fault.

The fragrance of lilies and roses scented the room and the evening sunshine created a golden glow that looked enchanting.

The luggage had been brought upstairs and the French lady's maid had already opened one of Madame's trunks.

Kezia could see at a glance that it was filled with extremely expensive clothes.

"I hope you will find everything – you want," she said to Madame de Salres.

She was walking around the room as if looking for something that she could find fault with.

As Madame did not reply, Kezia said to the lady's maid in French,

"If there is anything that Madame requires, please tell me. We will certainly do our best to provide it."

"*Merci, madame*, you are very kind," the lady's maid replied.

She was a middle-aged woman. Kezia thought that she seemed good-tempered and hoped that she would get on well with Humber and Betsy.

Having no wish to say anything more, she went from the room, closing the door behind her.

Outside in the corridor she realised that the door of the Water Lily Room was open and that the Marquis's valet, who looked exactly as she thought a Frenchman should look, was unpacking his Master's trunk.

She went into the room and said what she had said in French to the lady's maid,

"Good afternoon! I hope you will find everything your Master needs, but if not, please tell me."

The Frenchman rose to his feet and bowed.

"*Merci, madame.* I am used to accommodatin' Monsieur wherever we find ourselves."

Because he sounded so friendly, Kezia smiled at him and then remarked,

"You will understand that we live very quietly here and the servants are old, so, as I have already said, please come to me if there is anything you want and I will do my best to provide it."

The Frenchman thanked her again and, because he sounded so sincere and so sensible, she felt less anxious.

But still wondering if Perry required anything from her, she went downstairs again.

To her surprise he was not in the drawing room.

The Marquis was there alone, standing at the diamond-paned window and looking out onto the garden.

"I thought that my husband would be back," Kezia exclaimed.

"I hope he is admiring my horses," the Marquis replied. "I bought them only two days ago from an old friend, the Duke of Alderstone."

Kezia replied without thinking,

"I know the Duke has some very fine racehorses, but I am surprised that he sold you the fine team that you arrived with. I would have expected him to want them for himself."

The Marquis smiled.

"Shall I say that I made the offer so attractive that he found it impossible to refuse me?"

"Is that what you often do?" Kezia asked him curiously.

"When I want something, the price I pay for it is immaterial," the Marquis declared. "I am a Norman and I always get what I want."

Kezia sighed.

"It must be marvellous to be as rich as that. At the same time – too easy."

"What do you mean – *too easy?*" the Marquis enquired.

Kezia walked to the window and she was looking out at the garden, which, while bright with colour, looked very wild and unkempt.

"I spoke without thinking," she said after a moment's pause, "but I have learnt how hard it is to be without what one needs and loves, but it is also overwhelmingly exciting if one can achieve what one desires."

"I understand exactly what you are saying," the Marquis remarked, "but then what do you desire?"

Kezia nearly told him the truth and wanted to say,

'For you to buy the diamond necklace!'

Then she thought that it would be too revealing to say that and so she tried to think of something that would not depend on the money he would give them for it.

To her surprise he read her thoughts.

"Apart from the obvious answer that you are thinking about. What else?"

She blushed because he was so perceptive and then he said with a somewhat cynical note in his voice,

"Surely unlike most women you cannot say that you have everything? Or is it true in your case that true love is enough?"

For a moment Kezia did not understand what he meant.

Then she remembered that she was supposed to be Perry's wife and she replied quickly,

"You are right – of course you are right. If one has love – nothing else matters."

As she spoke, she looked at the Marquis and saw a growing expression in his eyes that she did not understand.

She had a feeling that this was just the sort of conversation that Perry had warned her about.

Hastily, because she was feeling embarrassed, she said,

"I must go and get ready for dinner and please, although I am sure that it is an incorrect thing to say – do not be late."

She thought that he looked surprised and added,

"I have taken so much trouble over the menu and, if the dishes are spoilt, it will be a disaster!"

The Marquis laughed and it was a spontaneous sound.

"I will not be late," he promised.

Because she felt that she was saying all the wrong things, she ran from the room, closing the door behind her.

Then, to her relief, she saw that Perry was coming in through the open front door.

"Is everything all right?" she asked.

"I have never seen such fine horses," Perry replied. "Have a look if you get the chance! I have somehow to make the Marquis agree that they need exercising tomorrow morning!"

Kezia drew in her breath before she said,

"Don't forget to remind him you have – a wife who – loves riding!"

She moved towards the staircase, saying as she did so,

"Don't be late for dinner, Perry. Remember you have to serve the wine. I have told Humber to do nothing more than bring in the dishes."

"I will not forget," Perry promised and walked towards the drawing room as Kezia ran up the stairs.

When she reached her bedroom, she thought that so far there had been no catastrophes, but she knew that she was feeling increasingly nervous about dinner.

She changed her clothes with lightning speed, finding that her mother's evening gown fitted her and was, if she had the time to look at herself, exceedingly becoming.

Clearly it was not as fashionable as anything that Madame de Salres would wear, but it made her skin look very white and she put on the only piece of jewellery she possessed.

It was a narrow black velvet ribbon that she had suspended a small pendant from.

It was not expensive, but a pretty one and, as her neck was long, she thought that the black velvet and the pendant made her look dignified.

Now there was no more time to think of her appearance, but only to concentrate on the dinner.

When she was dressed, she hurried to the kitchen to find out if there was anything that she could do for Betsy.

To her relief everything seemed to be in good order.

She had prepared the first course during the afternoon and also the second, which was four small trout that Perry had skilfully caught in the lake.

These she garnished with a French sauce and decorated them with slices of lemon, which made the whole dish look very attractive as well as eatable.

The bowl of soup that preceded it was of beetroot from the garden that grew without needing any attention. Her mother had taught her how to make Borscht, which was a Russian dish.

As she added the thick cream to the heated soup, she thought apprehensively of the very large bill they owed at the farm for everything that they had purchased for tonight's dinner.

When the soup was ready, she ran quickly to the drawing room and found to her relief that both the Marquis and Madame de Salres were there.

"Please don't think it unconventional," she said, "but, as our butler is very old and it is quite a long way to the dining room – I am telling you myself that dinner is ready!"

The Marquis put down the glass that he held in his hand.

"I am delighted to hear it!" he smiled.

Perry offered his arm to Madame de Salres.

"I 'ave not yet finished my champagne," she insisted coyly.

Kezia felt that she was just saying it to be awkward.

"Then allow me to carry it in for you," Perry replied.

There was nothing that Madame de Salres could do but put her hand on his arm as he picked up her glass and they then moved towards the dining room.

As the Marquis reached Kezia, who was standing by the door, he said,

"I have an idea, Lady Falcon, that this is the first dinner party you have given since you have been married."

"Why should you think – that?" Kezia asked.

"Because you are anxious for it to be a success and also a little apprehensive in case it is a failure."

Kezia laughed.

"I am only afraid because I feel that, as you are so particular. you will find our modest efforts at *haute cuisine* do not compare with those in your own country."

"I will answer that after dinner," the Marquis proposed, "and I have a feeling, and I am sure that I am not wrong, that you know quite a lot about *haute cuisine* as you call it!"

Kezia looked at him in surprise.

It was true that her mother had taught her to make the French dishes that her father so enjoyed.

As it so happened, when they were first married, they had spent a good deal of time in France and it was impossible for Betsy to tempt her father's palate.

Lady Falcon herself had therefore cooked the more difficult dishes for dinner and Kezia had always helped her, especially with the sauces.

With new candles in the silver candelabra, which were the only light in the room, the table looked glamorous and inviting

Kezia had even found time to decorate the centre of the table with flowers of different colours.

Perry poured out the wine and Humber came into the ding room with the plates of soup, which, fortunately, were still hot.

Kezia was almost too frightened for the moment to eat or even sip her glass of wine.

The Marquis finished his plate and stated,

"Delicious! I must congratulate you, Lady Falcon, on Course Number One!"

"You are making me nervous, *monsieur*!" Kezia protested with a smile.

She knew confidently as she spoke that there would be nothing at all wrong with Course Number Two.

It was then that Madame de Salres decided to fascinate and intrigue either the Marquis or Perry, Kezia was not sure which.

In a seductive voice that she had not used previously, she then flirted with both of them, holding each man completely captive so that there was no need for Kezia to speak.

Madame de Salres fluttered her eyelashes that were heavily mascaraed and made every word she spoke seem to have a *double entendre*.

She was not actually beautiful.

But Kezia realised that she was so fascinating that she could understand how Perry found it hard to keep his eyes off her.

She was not certain what the Marquis thought.

As she glanced at him and could see that there was a twinkle in his eyes, she thought that there was a sarcastic twist to his lips.

It was, Kezia thought towards the end of the meal, exactly like being on the stage.

They were all taking part in either a comedy or a drama in which the actors spoke witty provocative words written for them by somebody else.

She was quite happy to listen and realise with satisfaction that the Marquis was enjoying the dinner.

The roasted baby lamb with its accompanying vegetables was a typically English dish and she had made a cold *soufflé* exactly as her mother had taught her to do, which was very French and had a sauce that came from Paris.

There was no cheese, which Kezia knew was usually served at a French dinner. Instead she had provided an English savoury that was another of her father's favourites.

All Betsy had to do was to heat it up and again the Marquis finished everything that was on his plate.

He also seemed to enjoy the claret that Perry had served with the lamb and a Sauternes that was poured out with the *soufflé.*

Madame de Salres was whispering something to Perry that she obviously did not wish anyone else to hear and the Marquis turned to Kezia,

"Now you can relax! And may I commend you, my Lady, on the excellence of your dinner, which was quite superlative and the equal, if not better, than anything I have eaten in Paris."

"That may not be true," Kezia said, "but it makes me very happy to hear you say it."

"How have you learnt to cook so well?" the Marquis asked. "And don't pretend that an English cook could have managed all these dishes, each of which had something to me very recognisable in it."

"My mother taught me," Kezia explained. "My parents spent a great deal of their time in France."

As she spoke, she realised that she was speaking as if she was herself and added quickly,

"And I might say the same about my father and mother-in-law."

"I have always understood," the Marquis then remarked, "that the English disapproved of cousins marrying."

Kezia knew that he was thinking of the old adage that first cousins should never have children.

The idea made her shy and she blushed as she said quickly,

"We are second cousins and, as we have known each other since we were children, it was perhaps natural that we should fall in love."

"And, of course, you are very very much in love with your husband?"

As he spoke, he glanced at Perry, who was still captivated by Madame de Salres, who was saying something in a voice so low that neither he nor Kezia could hear her.

"Of course – I am!" Kezia replied firmly.

"And you have never been in love with anyone else?" the Marquis enquired.

"No – of course – not!"

Again she was speaking as herself and she added rapidly,

"We have always been together."

"And yet your husband goes to London," the Marquis said as if he was working it out. "I have seen him at several Race Meetings without you."

"I have – so much to do here," Kezia replied.

"Then you don't mind him being away? Perhaps enjoying himself without you?"

Because she thought that the Marquis was being far too inquisitive, Kezia suggested,

"I think that now Madame and I should leave you two gentlemen to your port."

She rose and for a moment Madame de Salres made no effort to leave the table.

Instead once again she was whispering something in Perry's ear that made him laugh.

Then, as if she suddenly realised that Kezia had risen to her feet, she cried,

"*Mon Dieu*! Always I forget about this primitive custom of the English of leavin' the gentlemen at the table!"

She put out her hand and laid it on Perry's.

"Don't be too long, *mon cher*, I so much prefer the conversation of men to the chitter-chatter of women!"

CHAPTER THREE

Kezia could not sleep.

She found herself going over and over everything in her mind and wondering if anything that would make the guests more comfortable had been forgotten or overlooked.

She had remembered that they would require drinking water in their bedrooms and she found that fortunately two of the little glass jugs her mother had always loved had remained unbroken.

She had also remembered to put out some Oil of White Violets for the bath in Madame de Salres's room. Her mother always distilled it at the same time as her perfume.

Douglas had carried cans of water up to both rooms and Kesia had instructed him to empty and remove the baths afterwards and to take away the bathmats.

She had slipped up the stairs before the others went to bed to make quite certain that their bedclothes were laid out correctly.

She had been amazed at Madame de Salres's very transparent nightgown.

Although it was indeed beautiful, she was sure that her mother would have considered it very immodest.

At least dinner had been a success and she could only pray that tomorrow night things would go off as smoothly. She knew what a strain it was on Betsy to have to make extra meals for more people than usual and in quick succession.

It was difficult for her to decide what she really thought of the Marquis.

He was so overwhelming and so much larger than she had expected not only physically, but mentally as well.

At the same time she had to admit that it had been really interesting to talk to him.

He was certainly very different from what she had imagined a Frenchman would be like.

Then she recalled what he had said when they were talking about the horses that he had bought from the Duke,

"I am a Norman and I always get what I want!"

A Norman!

Vaguely at the back of her mind she thought that this meant something different from the fact that he just came from Normandy.

She lay thinking about it, then, as she had always done, she decided that she must find out the right answer to her questions.

She jumped out of bed, put on the woollen dressing gown that she had worn for many years and cautiously opened her bedroom door.

Everything was very quiet and she reckoned that the guests and Perry would now be fast asleep.

She had deliberately left two sconces burning in the corridor as she thought perhaps it would seem very dark and perhaps frightening if either of their guests came out of their rooms.

There was no reason why they should do so, but the light made it easy for Kezia to go downstairs and along to the library.

It was a large room and the books were old, but she felt that she knew exactly where to find every one of them.

It took her only a few short seconds to put her hand on a copy of the *Encyclopaedia Britannica*.

When she wished to learn, she often thought how lucky she was that her grandfather, the 'Bad Baronet', had been so extravagant.

He had bought the *Encyclopaedia Britannica* when it was first published in 1768.

Now that more volumes had been added to it the first edition looked extremely old and tattered and the leather that covered it had lost its colour.

Kezia looked up Normandy and under a brief description of the region she found what she was seeking.

Then, because it seemed so fascinating, she gave an exclamation.

It had been the Vikings, Northmen or Normans, who had raided the coasts of Europe in the Emperor Charlemagne's time.

She read on and found that the most celebrated Norman Duke was Rollo, who was said to have died a pagan.

Even more fascinating was that his grandson became William the Conqueror, William I of England.

There was a great deal for Kezia to read in the *Encyclopaedia Britannica.*

The Normans first had been pagan destroyers bent on senseless plundering and slaughter, but, as the centuries passed, they converted to Christianity and became Knights.

Their men were still fierce, very strong and overpowering and Kezia felt that all these qualities applied to the Marquis.

It took her a long time to read it all, as there was so much to be said about the Normans.

In almost every country where they settled they had become leaders and rulers and, in many ways, they were a distinct law unto themselves.

They were so strong that a mere handful of Normans could vanquish an enemy many times more numerous and had, she read, an unequalled capacity for rapid movement across land and sea.

But their great courage and their instinct, which made them victorious however unlikely the odds, turned them into supermen who it would have been impossible not to admire and repect.

As she finished reading what had been written, Kezia gave a deep sigh. She was always very moved by anything she read and felt in a way that it became a part of herself.

Now she could not help thinking it was thrilling to have a real Norman staying with them in the house.

It was obvious that the Marquis by his blood stood head and shoulders above other men.

She put the *Encyclopaedia Britannica* carefully back onto its shelf.

Then she blew out the candle, knowing that she could easily find her way blindfolded back along the corridor into the hall and up the stairs to her bedroom.

She thought that tomorrow she would attempt to persuade the Marquis to talk to her about his ancestors and their exploits.

She had read that Bayeux was one of the places in Normandy that had been annexed by Duke Rollo and the Normans had settled there and it would be the home of the famous tapestry lauding the conquests of William I.

She reached the top of the stairs and she was just about to walk along the corridor back to her room when she was aware of a movement at the far end of it.

Instinctively she stopped.

Then she realised in the very faint light coming from one candle still alight in its sconce that the door of Madame de Salres's bedroom had opened.

It then flashed through Kezia's mind that perhaps, as Perry had suggested, she might be frightened.

In fact, earlier in the evening, when Madame de Salres had been talking to Perry, the Marquis had said to Kesia,

"What are you worrying about? I can see an anxious look in your eyes."

Kezia had laughed.

"I am not worrying about anything now that you have enjoyed your dinner."

"I very much appreciated it," the Marquis said, "and I ought to have thanked you for the flower arrangement on the table."

Kezia smiled.

"It was a pity that the only small flowers I could find were pansies."

"I have never seen them so well presented," the Marquis smiled, "and I imagine that you are also responsible for the flowers in this room and, of course, in my bedroom."

"I am sorry that there are so few water lilies," Kezia said, "but they are only just coming into flower."

"I thought they were like you," the Marquis remarked quietly.

Kezia, however, did not realise that he had paid her a compliment.

Instead she said,

"It was my – my-my – " she hesitated. "My mother-in-law who named all the bedrooms after flowers. I would like to have put Madame de Salres into the Rose Room so that I could decorate it with roses, but Perry thought that she should be in the Lilac Room and, of course, the lilac is now over."

"Why did your husband insist on that?" the, Marquis asked curiously.

"He felt that she might be upset or nervous in the night," Kezia explained, "and therefore would want to be near to you."

For a moment the Marquis looked surprised.

Then there was a faint smile on his lips that Kezia did not understand.

Now, as she saw him come from Madame de Salres's room, she thought that perhaps she had called him and he had gone to her assistance.

Then, as he walked into his own room and closed the door behind him for the first time she understood why Perry had claimed that it was insulting that he should bring Madame de Salres with him.

As the realisation of what he had meant swept over her, she was so shocked that she was unable to move.

She could only stare along the corridor at the two doors side by side and think that she must be mistaken.

That could not have been the reason why the Marquis had gone into Madame de Salres's bedroom.

Then she told herself that she was being very stupid.

Of course that was why Perry had been so insistent that she should go away.

That was why he had wanted to prevent her from meeting the Marquis just in case he should suggest to her that she should behave in the same manner as Madame de Salres.

'How could I ever do – such a – thing?' Kezia asked herself.

Now that the passage was empty, she ran as quickly as she could to her room and closed the door and locked it.

It was something that she could never remember doing before.

But she felt as if she must barricade herself in so that not only the Marquis but no other man could ever approach her in such a manner.

And yet, when she climbed back into bed and thought it over, it seemed somehow part of the Norman character.

She remembered reading how the Vikings, when they had invaded England had killed the men where they landed, ruined their crops and carried off their animals and their women.

She had wondered vaguely at the time why they had taken the women away and thought that perhaps they used them as slaves or cooks.

Now she could understand that they had a different reason for thrusting them into their longboats and taking them home.

She could imagine the Marquis doing the same, wearing a Viking helmet with horns and looking fierce and terrifying.

'Perry is right – he is a – bad man,' she murmured to herself, 'and the sooner he – buys the necklace and – leaves the better!'

She thought that if the necklace brought a curse upon him, it would be exactly what he deserved.

She wished that his visit were over and she would never have to see him again.

*

In the morning the sun was bright and everything seemed different.

When Perry found Kezia downstairs laying the table, he enthused,

"Your wish is granted and you had better go upstairs and change!"

"What are you saying?" Kezia asked him.

"The Marquis promised me last night that we could ride on his horses immediately after breakfast."

Kezia gave a little gasp.

"Oh, Perry, did he really say we could ride his horses?"

"We have a choice of six mounts, one of those ridden by the outriders won a gruelling Steeplechase last month and I am so astonished that the Duke agreed to part with him."

Once again Kezia could hear the Marquis saying,

"I am a Norman and I always get what I want."

She was, however, not prepared to argue but just be grateful for the moment when she could ride a horse that was really superb.

Her riding habit was rather worn, but the stiff lace-edged petticoat that went beneath it had been washed and starched.

So put on the blouse of white muslin, which been darned in several places and over it went a too tight-fitting jacket, which gave her, although she was not in the least aware of it, a most elegant figure.

She put on a small dark riding hat, which did not disguise the red in her hair.

By the time the Marquis and Perry had finished their breakfast, Kezia was waiting for them outside the front door.

She was patting and longing to mount one of the three glorious horses that the grooms had brought round from the stables.

Because of the shock of what she had learned the previous night, Kezia did not look at the Marquis as he came out into the sunshine to greet her,

"Good morning. Lady Falcon. I am glad you have decided to join your husband and me and I hope that my horse will not prove too obstreperous for you."

Kezia guessed that, because she was small and slight the Marquis thought that she would not be able to control a spirited animal.

There was no use in trying to explain that she had ridden since she could walk, so she merely said,

"Please, which horse may I ride?"

"I think you will find Thunderbolt, despite his name, the easiest," the Marquis replied.

Thunderbolt was the chestnut that Kezia had admired earlier and, as she went eagerly to his side, the Marquis lifted her deftly into the saddle.

For a moment, because he was touching her, she was conscious of a strange sensation that she did not understand but which, she told herself, was of repugnance.

She lifted the reins and, without waiting for the Marquis and Perry to mount the other horses, started off down the drive that led to the Park.

Thunderbolt was not at all tired after his journey of the previous day and he expressed himself by bucking several times and then moving more quickly than Kezia wished him to.

She managed to keep him under control and led the way through the Park, avoiding the low branches of the trees.

Then she was on the uncultivated ground where her father had always trained his horses and it was where she and Perry had galloped when they had horses to ride.

Now she had no intention of waiting for anybody.

She gave Thunderbolt his head, knowing as she did so that this was the most exciting thing that had happened to her for a very long time.

She must have ridden for nearly a mile before the Marquis and Perry caught up with her and she thought that her brother looked happier than she had seen him for a long time.

Now it was Perry's turn to lead the way and they jumped several low hedges and then rode into a field where there was a much higher hedge.

The Marquis, looking ahead, frowned and called out,

"I think, Lady Falcon, what lies ahead of us may be too much for you."

As she turned to answer, Kezia looked at him almost as if for the first time.

Never, she thought, had she seen a man look better on a horse or so much a part of it.

That he was a superlative rider went without saying. For the moment she could almost see him dressed in the heavy mail armour called hanbeck with a long broad-braided sword and a kite-shaped shield bearing down upon his enemy.

"This is the most exciting ride I have had for years!" she replied. "So please don't try to stop me!"

As she finished speaking, they had almost reached the tall hedge and, as Thunderbolt took it with almost a foot to spare, she laughed with sheer delight.

Then they were galloping side by side, taking the next hedge they came to and it was obvious that the Marquis was no longer worried about her riding ability.

Only when they turned for home was Kezia able to say,

"Thank you – thank you! I don't remember when I have – ever been so – happy!"

"I was about to say the same thing," Perry agreed, "and I only wish that I could afford horses the equal of these."

"I expect they are available if you look for them," the Marquis replied, "and I consider that those in my stables at home to be even better."

"Now you are boasting," Kezia sighed, "for I don't believe that any horse could be better than Thunderbolt."

"Then I see that this is something I shall have to prove to you," the Marquis answered, "but we will talk about it later."

She wondered what he meant and told herself that she really had no desire to talk to him.

He had shocked her and Perry had been absolutely right in warning her that he was the type of man she should not meet.

At the same time she had to admit that his horses and, if she was being honest, the man himself, had brought something new and unusual into her life.

When he was gone and she was alone again, she thought about how she would dream that she was riding Thunderbolt.

She would also, although she would indeed try not to, repeat in her mind everything that the Marquis had said to her.

'He is a Norman and Normans are pagans!' she thought despairingly.

She glanced at him and thought that it was impossible for any man to look so regal and so undoubtedly a conqueror.

"Your land needs cultivating," the Marquis turned to Perry unexpectedly.

"I realise that," Perry replied, "but for the moment I just cannot afford to farm it."

"Are you really so poor?" the Marquis then asked. "Your walls hold a great many fine pictures that are undoubtedly valuable."

"Find me one that is not entailed," Perry replied, "and I will be happy to sell it to you."

"I apologise," the Marquis exclaimed. "That was stupid of me. I had forgotten that the English entail everything onto their eldest son for generation after generation."

There was silence for some minutes and then the Marquis commented,

"At least I understand that the necklace I have come to see is saleable."

"Which, I can assure you, is very fortunate for me," Perry answered.

"Then we will look at it this afternoon," the Marquis proposed, "and, if you are not tired of riding, we can exercise my other three horses after luncheon."

Kezia gave a cry of delight.

"Oh, please," she begged, "do let's do that! When you leave tomorrow, I shall have only poor old Dobbin to ride and he is so slow that I can go more quickly on my own two feet."

The Marquis laughed.

"That is certainly a sad story and I am sure that it is something that your husband will be able to rectify."

Kezia knew that he was referring to the sale of the necklace and she said,

"Perry wants me to go to London to attend the balls and be presented to the Queen, but if I could have a horse like this one, I would much rather stay here and ride!"

"Then that is something you will have to wish for very hard," the Marquis suggested, "as I am sure you know, it is only by our own willpower that wishes come true."

"That is just what I want to believe," Kezia said, "but sometimes it is – difficult."

Then without thinking she added,

"It is so easy for you as you are a Norman and Normans have always been conquerors."

The Marquis looked amused.

"So you think that is what I am?"

"It is certainly in your blood."

"How do you know this?"

"I have been reading about the Normans in the *Encyclopaedia Britannica*," Kezia said truthfully.

"Were you interested in me or the Normans?" the Marquis asked.

She glanced at him and there was an expression in his eyes that made her look away again.

She then remembered what she had found out last night when she was returning from the library.

Without answering the question she just touched Thunderbolt with her whip and then she was galloping away.

And it was some time before the two men were able to catch up with her.

Luncheon was to be a light meal in order to save Betsy for the effort that she would have to make in preparing dinner.

Kezia hurried off to the kitchen as soon as they returned to the house.

She made the salad dressing and finished off the first course, which Betsy had already started on.

She added butter to the vegetables, which had been forgotten, and then found that she had no time to change her clothes.

She had taken off her riding hat and jacket and now she went into the dining room wearing her white muslin blouse and riding skirt.

She looked very young and, as it happened, very lovely, but she avoided the Marquis's eyes and said 'good morning' to Madame de Salres.

The contrast between her and the Frenchwoman was, Kezia thought, almost ludicrous.

Madame de Salres, who had just come from her bedroom, was wearing a gown, which boasted the voluminous skirt that had just come into fashion.

The pleating on the hem, the lace and the little touches of velvet, were all part of the genius of a French *couturier*.

Madame de Salres looked as if she had just stepped out of a picture frame.

She regarded Kezia first in surprise and then with a disdain that made her feel very small and insignificant.

Then, as if she was of no consequence, Madame flirted, as she had done last night, both with the Marquis and with Perry. She had an expertise that was unmistakably French.

Kezia made no effort to join in the conversation.

She knew that there was a great deal of it that she did not understand and the rest she did not want to.

She was vividly aware now that Madame de Salres was what the servants would call 'a scarlet woman' and she felt that her ancestors in their frames on the wall were looking down at her with disapproval.

She became suddenly aware that the Marquis was now staring at her and she had the frightening feeling that he could read her thoughts.

Quickly she said,

"You have not yet told us, *monsieur*, about your Château in Normandy. Is it a Norman Castle?"

"I am afraid not," the Marquis replied. "There was a Castle on the site several centuries ago, but it has been replaced by the Château, which I think you will admire when you see it."

This was something that was very unlikely, Kezia mused to herself.

With an effort she then said,

"My mother and father have – told me about the Châteaux of France and how beautiful they were before the dreadful Revolution. I believe, however, Normandy did not suffer any great damage."

"Certainly not as bad as in the centre of France and, of course, near Paris."

"You were lucky."

"I like to think I am," he replied, "and very lucky as well in coming here."

Again there was that expression in his eyes that made her feel shy and she said quickly,

"As you have finished luncheon, I think I will get ready to go riding so that I shall not keep you waiting."

"Ridin'?" Madame de Salres exclaimed. "You cannot mean you are goin' ridin' again? *Tiens*, Vere, 'ow can you be so ungallant and so unkind?"

"There are three horses for us to exercise," the Marquis remarked.

"'Orses! 'Orses!" Madame de Salres exclaimed. "We poor women will 'ave to grow four legs if we are to compete!"

"I can only say to you, *madame*," Perry came in, "that you manage very skilfully to eclipse everyone and everything with two!"

Madame de Salres smiled at him.

"Merci, *mon brave*! You are very kind and very encouragin', which is more than can be said for Monsieur le Marquis!"

She threw a provocative glance at the Marquis as if she was challenging him.

There was, however, a twist to the Marquis's lips as he replied,

"You know, Yvonne, you don't enjoy riding and therefore we look to you to entertain our hearts and our minds when we have exercised our bodies."

"I can easily think of other ways for you to do that!" Madame de Salres countered him provocatively.

The way she spoke made even Kezia understand what she meant.

She rose from the table rapidly saying in a voice that sounded loud and sharp even to herself,

"As luncheon is over, I think you would be more comfortable in the drawing room."

She walked to the door and, before the Marquis could open it for her, she had left the room and was moving quickly down the passage.

Kezia felt that Madame de Salres was, with her innuendoes, making her feel dirty.

'I hate her!' she told herself as she went up the stairs.

Then, as she reached her bedroom, she remembered that the Marquis had not yet seen the necklace.

If it was for Madame de Salres and she disparaged it, then perhaps he would not buy it.

'Help me – Mama – not to be – stupid over this,' she prayed, 'but it does – seem wrong and is spoiling – everything you made so beautiful.'

She knew as she put on her jacket and her hat that it might be the sensible thing not to accompany the Marquis and Perry this afternoon.

But the temptation of riding the Marquis's horses proved too strong for her to resist.

When she went downstairs, she found to her surprise that only the Marquis was waiting for her in the hall.

"Where is Perry?" she asked.

"Your husband is playing the perfect host," the Marquis replied, "and, as Madame de Salres does not wish to be left alone, he is taking her driving in his phaeton."

Kezia gave a little cry of horror.

"He should not do so! He enjoys riding your horses so much and he may never have the chance to do so again."

"I promise that he shall have the chance."

"But – how?" Kezia asked bluntly.

"I will answer that a little later and perhaps what you are really objecting to is that he is escorting Madame de Salres."

Without thinking Kezia replied,

"Oh, no, not if it amuses him. But I feel certain that he would rather be riding."

As she spoke, she thought that there was no point in arguing about it and Perry could do as he wished.

She therefore walked out through the front door and did not see the expression in the Marquis's eyes.

Having mounted their horses, they went the same way as they had gone in the morning.

Only when they had taken the higher fences and slowed their horses down to a walk did the Marquis say,

"I have seen many women ride, but I think without exception that you are better than any of them."

"If you are speaking the truth," Kezia replied, "then it is the most wonderful compliment I have ever been paid!"

"I find that hard to believe," the Marquis said, "just as, when you said this morning that it was the happiest time you have ever spent, it could not have been true."

"It *is* true!" Kezia answered him in a rapt little voice. "I never thought that I would ever ride such a marvellous horse or jump such high hedges with so little difficulty."

"Then I would have expected that the happiest time of your life would have been your Wedding Day!"

Too late Kezia felt that she had been over-enthusiastic.

"That – is something – different," she said a little lamely after a short pause.

"In what way?" the Marquis asked.

Kezia could not think of a suitable reply and after a moment he said,

"You puzzle and bewilder me and at the same time I find you very intriguing!"

Because what he said was so surprising, Kezia turned round to look at him and found once again that the expression in his blue eyes made her feel shy.

"I think we – should be – going back," she said.

"You cannot always run away," the Marquis remarked.

"Who says I am doing so?"

"It is what you *are* doing," he answered, "and it is something I want to prevent."

"I cannot think why."

"As I have said, you intrigue me. You are very different from any Englishwoman I have ever known, just as your undeniable beauty is so different."

"I am sure that is – something you have said to a – hundred women," Kezia replied lightly.

The Marquis frowned.

"You are well aware that I am speaking the truth. Just as I can read your thoughts, you can read mine and you know that I am not flattering you."

Kezia looked at him in astonishment and for several moments her eyes were held by his.

Now she could read his thoughts quite clearly and she knew that they were somehow speaking to each other without words.

Then she responded,

"Please – Perry warned me about you – and now you are – frightening me!"

"Because I am not what you expected?" the Marquis asked.

"I think it is – because you are a – Norman and I have – never met anybody like you – also because – if you think I am different – you are – very very different!"

"You are different," the Marquis persisted quietly, "because I understand exactly what you are saying, just as you understand me without there being any need for explanations."

"B-but – there is – there *must* be!" Kezia said. "And it is a – mistake for us to – talk like this."

"What you are really thinking," the Marquis replied, "is that you are frightened because we think alike and it is quite comprehensible to us both."

It was not what he said but the depth of his voice.

Yet she realised that he was speaking sincerely and there was nothing flirtatious behind his words.

Because she was suddenly at a loss and also afraid of her own feelings, Kezia ran away.

She rode home as quickly as she could, aware that the Marquis was beside her and yet she neither looked at him nor spoke a word.

His servants were waiting for them outside the front door.

As she brought her horse to a standstill, Kezia slipped down from the saddle and, without waiting for the Marquis, ran up the steps and into the hall.

The staircase was in front of her.

But before she could reach it the Marquis caught hold of her arm and turned her round to face him.

"Why should you run away?" he asked in his deep voice.

"I have – already given – you the answer to that!"

"That you are frightened? But why? Think of it not as something physically frightening but as if we have suddenly reached the top of a high mountain or crossed a desert towards the horizon only to find that there is another one beyond it."

Now he had a hand on each of Kezia's shoulders and it was impossible for her to move.

She felt as if he was hypnotising her by what he was saying and she was also tinglingly aware that he was touching her.

For a long moment he gazed at her.

Then he said,

"Run and go on running! But, remember, as a Norman, I shall catch you and there is no escape!"

Then, as she stared at him and understanding what he was saying, but trying hard not to, he turned and walked away.

With a superhuman effort then Kezia ran up the stairs towards her bedroom.

*

Perry did not say anything when he came back from his drive with Madame de Salres.

Nor did he seem to mind in the slightest having missed another opportunity of riding one of the Marquis's magnificent horses.

Instead he looked rather pleased with himself, Kezia thought.

However, Madame de Salres looked at the Marquis defiantly, as if she had scored a point off him.

They had gone to the drawing room at four o'clock for English tea.

Kezia thought that it was one way of keeping them entertained whether they wanted to drink it or not.

The Marquis, however, ate the cucumber sandwiches and said he enjoyed them, while Madame de Salres sipped a little tea from a china cup and made a grimace.

Perry ate as if he was hungry and Kezia knew that he was really waiting for the moment when he would bring in the necklace.

Finally the Marquis finished his cup of tea and turned to Perry,

"Now, Falcon, where is this treasure that you have promised to show us? And I am sure that Yvonne will want to hear the story of how the Comtesse de la Motte managed to cause the greatest scandal that France has ever known."

"*Tiens*! I 'ave 'eard it before," Madame de Salres remarked, "and I 'ave always thought 'ow foolish she was to be found out!"

The Marquis chuckled.

"That, of course, is the Eleventh Commandment, '*Thou shalt not be found out*!' and those who break it must undoubtedly pay the penalty."

"At least she then managed to salvage something from ze wreckage," Madame de Salres went on, "so let us see ze necklace and find out if, after all 'er intriguin', it was worthwhile."

"I am sure it was not!" Kezia commented. "She was taken to prison and, having escaped to London, she could never return to her native land, so she died in exile."

"I am sure she must 'ave consoled 'erself with some 'andsome Englishman," Madame de Salres laughed.

She looked at Perry as she spoke and there was no doubt that he found her very alluring and the expression in his eyes was very obvious.

Kezia did not seem concerned and after a moment the Marquis asked,

"Well, where is the necklace? We are all waiting."

Perry rose rapidly to his feet.

"I will go to fetch it."

He went to his bedroom, where Kezia knew that he kept the necklace hidden in a secret place known only to the reigning Baronet.

Actually she knew it too because Perry had shown her where it was, so that if necessary she could move the necklace to another hiding place when he was away.

Now, as they waited in the drawing room, Madame de Salres threw out her long-fingered hands towards the Marquis as she said,

"Have you missed me, my charmin' unpredictable *cher ami*?"

"But of course," the Marquis replied without taking her hand.

"Then perhaps, if you will ask me very nicely, I will forgive you for being so unkind to me last night."

She spoke in French, as if she thought that Kezia would not understand and the Marquis replied in the same language,

"I think it is something we should discuss when we are alone."

~83~

Madame de Salres gave a little laugh.

"You don't imagine that these English, who are so insular that they never learn another language, can understand?" she queried. "But as you say, when we are alone I will pardon you for what you did not do while I would much prefer to show my gratitude for what you did do!"

It was now very obvious to Kezia what she was saying.

Quite suddenly, because she realised that the Marquis had not made love to Madame de Salres the night before, she felt unexpectedly happy.

The sun coming through the window was suddenly brilliant and she thought that she could hear the birds singing in unison.

Then she asked herself how it was possible that she could understand.

Yet whether she was reading the Marquis's thoughts or not, she knew that last night, while he had gone to say 'goodnight' to Madame de Salres, he had not made love to her.

Because Kezia was very innocent and had lived such a quiet life, she had no idea what a man did when he made love to a woman.

She knew that something happened which could be very wonderful.

At the same time without love it would also be primitive, frightening and even revolting.

She was aware that Royalty made arranged marriages as well as the aristocratic families of England and, of course, in France.

Because her father and mother had married for love, she had always imagined that it was something that would happen to her one day.

Somehow, although it was difficult to think how, she would meet the man of her dreams.

To marry for money or for position was something so unthinkable that it never occurred to her at any time.

What she could not understand was why men pursued women they had no wish to marry. They apparently made love to them even though they could never mean anything special in their lives.

It was a delicate subject that she had not wasted much thought on because it seemed so incomprehensible.

Yet last night when she had been shocked by the Marquis coming from Madame de Salres's bedroom, she had felt a revulsion against anything that was so wrong and improper.

It was as well, although she could not quite understand it, so ugly.

Now she knew why Madame de Salres had been flirting with Perry. Maybe, as she had said herself, she was punishing the Marquis for what he had not done last night.

Kezia had no idea how expressive her face was as she thought over what had just been said.

Then Perry came back into the room.

He was carrying in his hand a large leather box.

As he reached the Marquis, he lifted the lid and then handed the box to him.

Lying on black velvet was the famous necklace made of twenty-one large diamonds that had been stolen from the huge necklace intended for Queen Marie-Antoinette.

As the stones flashed and shone in the sunshine, they seemed dazzling and quite out of this world.

For a moment there was complete silence until Madame de Salres spoke up, her voice full of greed,

"It is beautiful! *Magnifique*! Oh, Vere, *mon cher*, my marvellous lover, give it to me!"

Her voice seemed to break the spell that had held the Marquis silent.

Then he looked at the Frenchwoman with a hardness in his eyes that made him, Kezia thought, seem more overwhelming and more awe-inspiring than he had ever been before.

Slowly he closed the lid of the box.

"No," he said and he seemed almost to drawl the words.

"No, this is not for you!"

CHAPTER FOUR

For a moment there was complete silence.

Then Madame de Salres gave a shrill scream.

"'Ow can you be so unkind to me, so 'eartless?" she asked him, her words tumbling over themselves. "I gives you my love, my 'eart, and you will not even give to me this necklace!"

The Marquis did not reply and, as if overcome by her feelings, she then swept out of the room, still screaming as she did so of his cruelty and unkindness.

As she went, she left three people staring after her in amazement.

Then the Marquis said in a quiet tone,

"I am certainly prepared, Falcon, to buy this necklace from you, but on one condition."

Kezia felt her heart almost miss a beat.

She was sure that the Marquis was going to say that it was too expensive, in which case perhaps Perry would refuse to sell him the necklace and hoping to find another purchaser.

If that happened, how could they possibly pay the bills they owed or continue to live in the house?

"Condition?" Perry questioned.

There was no doubt that he too was perturbed, but the Marquis had opened the leather box again and was looking at the necklace.

"I want this," he said, "for a Museum on my estate that will contain mementos of the French Revolution."

He paused before he went on,

"The Museum, of course, includes furniture, pictures and *objets d'art* from the reign of King Louis XV."

Kezia was listening intently, but she was still holding her breath.

"Of course this necklace would be a very important exhibit," the Marquis said, "and I will pay the sum you are asking for it."

With difficulty Kezia stifled a cry of delight.

She knew, without even looking at him, that Perry, who had been very tense, was now relaxed.

"What is the condition?" he asked after a long pause.

"Because I wish to have the setting altered," the Marquis explained, "in order to make it a little more impressive than it is at present, I cannot take it with me when I return to France next week. Instead I want you and your wife to bring it with you when you come to stay with me on the tenth of June."

"The tenth of June?" Perry repeated almost stupidly.

The Marquis smiled.

"I am arranging a Race Meeting that I know that you would like to participate in and I also thought, as these new horses jump so well, that I would organise a Steeplechase as well."

Perry's whole face seemed to light up.

Then, as Kezia made a little sound, he suddenly remembered her.

"It is something I should enjoy enormously," Perry smiled. "At the same time I think it will be impossible for Kezia to accompany me, as I know that she has commitments here that will prevent her from leaving."

The Marquis snapped the leather case shut and put it down on the small table beside the chair where Perry was sitting.

"In which case," he stipulated, "and, of course, I do understand how busy your wife is, I will however have to deny myself the pleasure of adding the necklace to my collection."

He rose to his feet as he spoke and started to walk towards the door.

Perry looked frantically at Kezia, whose face had gone very pale.

For a moment her voice seemed to have died in her throat and then, when the Marquis had almost reached the door, she called out,

"Wait – please – *wait*! I do have – as Perry has said – some previous engagements – but I am sure that I can – cancel them."

Her words seemed to tumble over themselves and slowly the Marquis turned back.

"You are quite sure you can do so?" he asked.

"Quite – q-quite – s-sure," she stammered.

Then, as her eyes met his, she knew that he had been certain from the very beginning of the conversation that he would get his own way.

Once again he was the victor, the conqueror, a Norman who was never ever defeated.

*

Because she felt exhausted by the drama of what had just happened, Kezia walked up the stairs slowly to her bedroom.

Sitting down in a chair by the window, she put her hands over her face.

They had won!

They had obtained the fortune that Perry had asked for the necklace, but at the same time everything seemed more complicated than it had been when the Marquis had first arrived.

How could she possibly go to France and stay in the Marquis's Château pretending to be Perry's wife?

What was she to do at the moment about Madame de Salres, who, shut in her bedroom, was still hysterical?

She tried to tell herself that nothing mattered except that the dark cloud of debts and despair had been lifted from over their heads.

Now she could do everything that had been left undone and a great deal more besides.

'First we must pay Humber and Betsy their wages, which are so long overdue,' Kezia reasoned. 'Secondly we must repair the cottages for the pensioners, help the farmers and put into cultivation the fields nearest to the house.'

Then she thought of the roof, the windows and the stove in the kitchen.

There were a thousand other things before she remembered that now she would be able to afford to buy a horse.

She rose to her feet to gaze out of the window.

As she did so, she thought that she could already see the garden tidy and cared for and looking as it had when she was a child.

The door of her bedroom suddenly opened and, as she turned round, Perry came into the room.

"I have it!" he bellowed triumphantly waving a cheque in his hand.

He walked across to her, put his arms around her shoulders and hugged her.

"We are rich!" he asserted. "*Rich*, Kezia, and it is all due to you! I am quite sure that if the Marquis had not enjoyed himself with us so much, he would have gone away without the necklace."

"But – we have to – take it to – him," Kezia said in a low voice.

"I know that," Perry replied, "but I would take it down into Hell rather than lose the sale. I was only trying to do what is best for you."

"I realised that," Kezia pointed out, "and it will be very – embarrassing to have to – pretend when we are – in France that we are – married."

"We will not stay long," Perry said reassuringly. "The race will take place the day after we arrive and we can leave the day after it is over."

Kezia wanted to say that there was so much to see that having reached France it would be a pity to have to leave too quickly.

But she thought it unwise to argue about it with Perry at this particular moment.

"I shall have to – buy some – new clothes," she said, "although I may be able to – alter one or – two of Mama's gowns."

"You shall have the gowns you have been owed for a long time," Perry promised her.

"Thank you very much, dearest. But remember, the money will not – last for – ever!"

She hesitated and then she added,

"Please, Perry, don't – gamble with any of it!"

"I am not such a fool as that," he answered, "and I don't intend to go to London until after we come back from France. There is a great deal here for me to do."

Kezia pushed away her doubts and thought that she must be as enthusiastic and happy as her brother was.

Perry was looking at the cheque he held in his hand as if he could hardly believe that it was real.

And then he said to her,

"Oh, by the way, I had forgotten, but the Marquis thought that there was still time before dinner for you to show him the house. He particularly wants to see the bedrooms because I told him that the four-poster in my bedroom came originally from Cornwall and apparently he is most interested in the carving."

"I expect he is comparing it with what the craftsmen produce in Normandy," Kezia said and then asked her brother, "where is he?"

"I left him in the library where he went to write out this cheque."

He looked at it again and added,

"We really ought to frame this and exhibit it in the same way as the Marquis will show off the necklace!"

Kezia laughed.

"Put it quickly in the bank so that we can draw out the money as we need it, otherwise it may fly away and you will find that we only imagined it."

"Don't say anything so terrible," Perry admonished her in mock horror, "and go now and do what the Marquis wants."

He paused for a moment.

Then he went on, almost as if he spoke to himself,

"I wonder if I ought to try to placate Yvonne?"

Kezia looked at him in surprise.

"No, of course not! She is in her bedroom!"

Perry hesitated.

Then he nodded,

"That is right and I expect she will recover when the Marquis gives her more jewels to add to the large collection that she has accumulated already."

Kezia looked at Perry wide-eyed.

"Are you saying that the Marquis gave her all those wonderful jewels that she has been wearing while she has been here?"

"I expect so. Rich men always have to pay heavily for their amusements."

Once again Kezia felt shocked.

It seemed just incredible that anyone would spend so much on one woman for what Perry called 'amusement'.

Because it was a subject that she did not wish to discuss with her brother, she walked towards the door, saying,

"I will show the Marquis the four-poster. And I hope your room is tidy."

"I doubt it," Perry replied.

Kezia then went downstairs to the library and found the Marquis with the *Encyclopaedia Britannica* in his hands.

He looked up as she approached him and said with an amused note in his voice,

"Now I see what you have been reading about me! Do you really think I am a primitive pagan, ruthless and overpowering?"

"You have not read far enough," Kezia replied. "You forget that the Normans, having started like that, became Christians and later Knights."

"But they were still conquerors."

"Of course – as undoubtedly you are!"

"I wonder," he said. "Perhaps some things are unobtainable."

"That does not sound like a Norman speaking," Kezia replied teasingly. "I am sure that they were never faint-hearted when they went into battle, but completely and absolutely sure that they would always be victorious."

"So that is what you want me to be?" the Marquis asked.

He was looking at her and suddenly she thought that there might be an innuendo in what they had been saying to each other.

Quickly, because she thought that he might know what she was thinking, she said,

"I want you to fight for what is right and what is good and what will – help other – people."

"And what about ourselves?"

"What could give you more satisfaction than knowing that you are battling against evil?"

"It depends on what you would call evil," the Marquis reflected quietly.

Kezia had the idea that they were duelling with words. Once again she could see him in his chainmail armour, his shield in one hand and a light spear in the other.

She could see him so vividly that she was not surprised when the Marquis broke into her thoughts,

"That is a fanciful picture that you are looking at. I am also a man, Kezia!"

She gave a little laugh as it seemed so ridiculous that he could translate her thoughts.

Then she replied,

"A man, but always a Norman and much more is therefore expected of you."

Then before the Marquis could reply to her and because she had the feeling that she was moving onto dangerous ground, she changed the subject,

"Perry said that you – wanted to see the bed that – his ancestors have slept in since before the time of William the Conqueror's invasion of England."

"It is possible that the bed could last so long?" the Marquis asked in a very different voice from the one that he had used before.

"I think perhaps its age has been somewhat exaggerated," Kezia admitted, "but it is very old, so do come and look at it."

They walked up the stairs side by side and it struck her that they might be climbing the mountain that he had referred to before.

"That would be harder!" he observed.

Kezia laughed.

"If you keep reading my thoughts, there will be no need for me to say anything to you at all and we can just sit in silence."

"As long as I am with you," the Marquis said, "it does not really matter what we do."

The way he spoke made Kezia feel as if her heart turned a somersault.

She hurried along the corridor to where the bedrooms were.

At the far end of it there was the room that had been the Master's ever since the house had been built.

It was a bit larger than all the other State Bedrooms and there were four diamond-paned windows in it besides a large open fireplace where it was possible to burn half a tree!

The beams of the ceiling were expertly carved and two of the walls were panelled.

But it was impossible to look at anything but the huge four-poster.

It was of oak and carved with animals, people and ships, all things familiar to the ancient craftsmen. It was not very high, but wide and surmounting the front of it was the Falcon crest with its Latin motto carved beneath it.

Kezia's mother had added new curtains of crimson velvet and had embroidered a velvet bedcover with the Falcon Coat of Arms.

She had done the work most skilfully and with love and it had taken her nearly two years to complete it.

While the rest of the room was somewhat shabby, the bedcover and the curtains seemed to glow almost as if a special light made them do so.

The Marquis stood looking at the four-poster for a long time before he commented,

"It is different in every way from anything I have seen before and I have a great deal of unique carving to show you when you come to my Château."

"I loved this room when I was a child," Kezia told him, "and I used to look out of the windows at the ducks as well as the rabbits and the squirrels that you can find peeping from between the trees."

"So you were here as a child?"

Kezia started and then remembered that she had been speaking as herself.

"Yes, of course," she replied quickly. "I often came to stay here with my parents."

Because she was lying, she looked away from the Marquis, afraid that his intuition where she was concerned would tell him that she was not speaking the truth.

He looked again around the room.

Then he observed,

"It is a very masculine room and there appears to be no trace of you in it, which I would have expected to find."

Kezia thought quickly.

"I sleep in a different room because Perry snores and also, because I am here alone so much, I find my own room cosier and perhaps with not so many ghosts in it!"

"I would very much like to see your room," the Marquis suggested.

Kezia thought that this was a mistake, but she could think of no reason for refusing his request.

She walked towards the door, saying,

"First I would like to show you the other rooms."

She opened the door of the room next to Perry's.

"This was my – my mother-in-law's room."

Even as she entered it, she wondered why she had taken the Marquis, of all people, into the room that she had always thought of as a very special shrine to her mother.

But it was too late now to go back.

She pulled aside the curtains so that he could see a very different bed from the one that they had been looking at in the Master's bedroom.

This was a four-poster here too and it was also carved, but it was gilded and the posts had a very delicate design and at the top of the bed there were small cupids carrying garlands of flowers.

The Marquis looked round the room in silence for some time until at last he said,

"This is a room of love and I find it strange that you don't sleep in it!"

"I left it as it was when my – mother-in-law was alive," Kezia replied.

She moved quickly from the room and there was nothing that the Marquis could do but follow her.

She showed him the Rose Room and then she came to her own bedroom.

As she put out her hand towards the door, she hesitated and remarked,

"I am sure it will soon be time for us – to dress for dinner."

"I have not yet seen your room," the Marquis objected at once.

He spoke quietly, but Kezia felt a force behind the words that commanded her to do what he wished.

Because he somehow made her feel helpless, she opened the door and he could see the room that she had slept in ever since she was a child.

The bed was not elaborate or carved as in the other rooms. It was draped in white muslin and the curtains fell from a small corolla almost like a halo that was attached to the ceiling.

Her dressing table also had what the servants called 'a muslin petticoat' round it and the curtains were draped with a frill and they were caught back on each side of the window with a rope covered in silk flowers.

It was a very lovely and tranquil room.

Because she was so much alone and spent more time in it than anywhere else in the house, Kezia had moved the pictures she that liked best to hang on the walls.

Now she realised for the first time that they were all French and she had chosen them because they had some spiritual meaning for her that was difficult to put into words.

As the Marquis looked at them, she sensed that he understood and waited to hear what he had to say.

She thought that he would never speak and then, when he did, he said quietly,

"I would have known that this was your room even if I had come here alone!"

With that he walked over to the door, opened it, passed through and closed it behind him, leaving Kezia inside.

*

As she dressed for dinner, Kezia felt apprehensive in case Madame de Salres continued to make a scene over the necklace.

But when she came downstairs, the Frenchwoman was all smiles and charm.

She flirted with Perry again and at the same time she was polite and more pleasant to Kezia than she had been since she had first arrived.

Kezia felt certain that it was something that the Marquis had said to her or done for her.

Whatever it was, she was grateful that there were to be no more dramatic demands for the necklace while she and Perry were present.

Dinner, as might have been expected, was not as good as it had been the previous night.

This was due, Kezia thought guiltily, to the fact that she had not spent as much time in the kitchen as she should have done.

But at least the food was edible and fortunately no one complained about anything.

Because Perry was in such a good humour, they all seemed to be laughing and enjoying themselves.

Madame de Salres held the table by fascinating both the men with an expertise that Kezia could never even attempt to emulate.

Then somewhat later, when they had moved to the drawing room, Madame de Salres and Perry walked through the French windows into the Rose Garden.

This left Kezia alone with the Marquis.

Because it was uppermost in her mind, she began,

"I want to thank you for buying the – diamond necklace. It will make all the difference to Perry – and to a great number of other people. Since they are unable to thank you themselves – I will do it for them."

"And that will make you happy?" the Marquis enquired.

"Very – very happy. It has become more and more difficult to keep – things going – wondering where the next penny is to – come from."

"But your husband goes to London," the Marquis said reflectively, "and enjoys a social life that most people would find very expensive."

"Perry is asked for himself – and does not have to – extend hospitality in return," Kezia explained a little lamely.

"While you are content to stay here?"

"I shall be more than content," Kezia replied, "now that you have so – generously bought – the necklace."

"I would like to be even more generous," he said, "but I feel that it is something you will not allow me to be."

Kezia looked up at him in some surprise and he saw by her expression that she did not understand.

"When you come to France. I wish to give you one of my horses and you will have quite a good number to choose from."

For a moment the expression on Kezia's face was dazzling and then she replied,

"No – no – of course – not. It is – generosity that I could not – accept."

"Why not?"

"Because it – would be – incorrect."

"And you think that your husband might be jealous?"

"No – not – jealous," Kezia said without thinking, "but envious."

"Then, of course, I shall have to give him one too."

"No – no. I did not mean that – of course I did – not mean that. In any case you have given us – quite enough – already and we could not possibly – presume on you for anything else."

She thought as she spoke of how shocked her mother would have been at the idea of any man giving her such an expensive present as a horse.

Before the Marquis could say anything, she added,

"Please – forget you made – such a suggestion – for I am sure that your horses – which are French – would be much happier in their own – country than in an alien land."

"As a Norman," he smiled, "I consider myself partly English and, as a conquered person, as you tell me that your ancestors fought at the Battle of Hastings, I think you will have to obey me and do as I tell you."

Kezia laughed.

"Nobody would think that was – a very logical argument."

"It is logical enough for me to insist that you choose a horse among those in my stables, but we will talk about it when you come to the Château Bayeux and I can have the pleasure of returning your hospitality, which I have enjoyed more than I can possibly say."

Because of the way he spoke, the very air seemed to be vibrating around them.

As she suddenly felt nervous, Kezia said,

"I do hope Madame de Salres does not catch cold. Even though it is summer, there can still be a chill wind in the evening."

"I can assure you Yvonne can look after herself, as she has already managed to do," the Marquis said cynically, "and then your husband will undoubtedly prevent her from feeling chilled!"

Now there was a definite note in his voice that made Kezia feel that he was annoyed with Perry and she said quickly,

"Perry always – tries to be the – perfect host, and Madame is very very attractive!"

"When I brought her here," the Marquis went on, "I had no idea that Sir Peregrine was married and I was aware the moment I saw you that I had made a mistake."

Because he was apologising, Kezia felt embarrassed.

"Please don't – think like that," she said. "Madame is so beautiful, so fascinating and so elegantly dressed – I know how different I look and you – must find, it – very boring."

"Do you really think that anything we have said or done since I have been here could possibly be described as boring?" the Marquis asked.

Now there was a deep note in his voice that seemed to vibrate through Kezia in a strange way.

"I am – expressing myself – very badly," she replied, "but I think – you understand."

"I do understand," the Marquis answered, "but I don't know quite what I can do about it and, God knows, that is something I have never said before in my whole life."

Kezia looked at him in surprise.

Then, when she was about to ask him for an explanation, Madame de Salres and Perry returned from the garden.

Eagerly, as if she was a young girl, the Frenchwoman then ran across the room to the Marquis.

She almost threw herself against him as she said in French,

"It is so romantic outside in the moonlight and under the stars. Come and look at them with me, Vere, and you will feel as you did when we first met that magical night in Paris."

She looked up at him as she spoke, and Kezia thought it would be impossible for him not to be captivated by Madame de Salres' pleading eyes and parted red lips.

She was aware that Perry, who had just come in behind her, was looking at her with an expression on his face that she had never seen before.

Suddenly she thought how insignificant and tongue-tied she was compared to a woman who could hold both men captive with her inexpressible fascination.

Because she felt unwanted, Kezia walked towards the door.

As she reached it, she heard Madame de Salres saying, again in French,

"Please come out with me, my most adorable, irresistible Vere!"

The way she spoke made Kezia feel as if a thousand knives were being plunged into her breast.

When she reached the hall, she started to run and kept on running until she reached her bedroom.

She flung herself down on the bed and as she did so she asked what was wrong and why she should feel as she did.

Then she was afraid of knowing the answer.

*

"So that is that!" Perry remarked as the Marquis drove off down the drive.

His two outriders followed behind and Madame de Salres's feathers were fluttering in her *chic* and extremely becoming bonnet.

"They – professed that they – enjoyed themselves," Kezia replied in a small voice.

"I certainly enjoyed having them," Perry commented, "and now I am driving straight to the Bank to deposit this cheque and draw out enough money for the wages and improvements that I intend to put in hand immediately."

"That sounds wonderful," Kezia tried to enthuse.

She was wondering as she spoke why she did not feel more elated.

Now that the Marquis and his followers were out of sight, the drive, curving away under the oak trees, seemed somehow empty.

"How could we have imagined for one moment that everything would go off so well?" Perry asked.

"Yes – we were very – lucky indeed," Kezia agreed.

Perry turned and walked back into the house.

"You will have to hurry and buy some new gowns," he urged. "There is only a little over two weeks before we leave for France."

"Suppose I fall – ill at the – last moment?" Kezia suggested in a low voice. "It would then be too – late for the Marquis to – cancel his cheque."

"Oh, for God's sake," Perry said sharply, "you don't want to play tricks with him. He might well ask for a refund on what we have already spent. Besides you will enjoy going to France. Why are you making such a fuss about it?"

"I-I am not," Kezia replied. "It is – just that – "

She stopped.

How could she possibly explain to Perry that she had been quite certain in her mind, although she had no proof of it, that last night the Marquis had gone to Madame de Salres's bedroom and made love to her.

Just as she had been able to read his thoughts, she was quite sure that this was what had happened.

It was why Madame de Salres had come down to dinner in such a good temper.

It was also why she had begged him to go out with her in the moonlight.

Perhaps he had promised to marry her and Kezia felt that it would be a real triumph if she could bring it off.

Perry left her to go to the stables to help get his horses ready so that he could drive his phaeton to the Bank.

Kezia then asked herself why she felt so depressed.

It was easier to say that it was the reaction from having so much to do than to face the truth.

Then she remembered how Perry had tried to prevent her from coming in contact with the Marquis in the first place.

His friend Harry had told him how irresistible to women he was and how they invariably behaved like lunatics because they had fallen in love with him.

'That is how I am behaving,' Kezia accused herself, 'and how can I torture – myself by going – to France?'

She recognised that there was no answer.

As Perry had said, the Marquis was so unpredictable that he might easily demand some of his money back. Alternatively by some clever means he might manage to cancel the whole transaction.

'I must not offend him – I must not,' she told herself.

Then a few minutes later she was being even more positive with herself,

'I don't – love him! I don't! How could I love anyone who is – ruthless and a Norman?'

The answer was quite simple, but she refused to acknowledge it.

Her whole body vibrated to his.

Having said 'goodbye', he had raised her hand to his lips and had actually kissed it. Just for a second she had felt the warmth of his mouth on her skin and it was as if a shaft of light had run through her whole body.

Because her hand trembled in his, she knew that he was aware of it.

Then, despite her resolution not to, she had looked into his eyes and there was nothing else in the world but him.

Finally she went into her mother's room.

The curtains had not yet been pulled back from the windows since she had been there yesterday with the Marquis.

'What can I – do about him – Mama?' she asked and knew that there was no answer to her question.

She went into the wardrobe room next door and wondered which of her mother's gowns she could take with her to France.

It would be a waste of their precious money to spend it on clothes when there were so many other things that had to be bought first.

Then she realised that one part of her mind was telling her to look as lovely as she could for him.

Then, as she thought of Madame de Salres in her exquisite gowns, she wanted to laugh at herself for her pretentiousness.

How could the Marquis possibly admire anyone so countrified, so unsophisticated and so foolishly innocent as she was?

She remembered how she had never understood the innuendoes that punctuated Madame de Salres's conversation.

Everything she had said seemed to make Perry and the Marquis laugh, while she had listened to them in bewilderment.

She must have seemed to be like a child dining for the first time with the grown-ups but unable to take part in or understand what they were saying.

She looked helplessly in her mother's wardrobes and then closed the doors.

'We will be there for only two nights,' she thought. 'So I will buy perhaps one evening gown that is more or less fashionable and something to go to the races in.'

She sighed and went on,

'But I will not be extravagant and I will ask one of the women in the village to help me with the alterations to Mama's dresses.'

She could do them quite ably herself, but she thought that there were so many other things for her to do.

She was sure that as soon as Perry had given his orders, there would be workmen in the house and they would have to be supervised and prevented from upsetting Humber and Betsy with the noise and mess they made.

'If I had any sense,' she reflected, 'I would have gone into the town with Perry and then I could have done some shopping while he was at the Bank.'

Then she told herself that the little Market town near where they lived would only have gowns that would look frumpish in France.

"It would be much – better if I could – stay here!" she said aloud.

Even as she spoke and the words seemed to echo in the silence all around her, she knew that she wanted to see the Marquis again.

She wanted to be with him and she wanted to hear him talking to her.

She wanted to see that expression in his eyes, which gave her that very strange sensation in her breasts.

At last she spoke the words aloud that seemed to be beating within her heart.

"I love – him! *I love – him* – but please – God, help me to try to – forget him!"

CHAPTER FIVE

As they neared the Château Bayeux, Kezia was convinced that she was dreaming.

When they had boarded the Marquis's luxurious yacht at Southampton, she had been certain then that she was now playing a part in a Fairytale.

So much had happened that she had begun to think that the past was no longer real and she was already living her life in the future.

When the Marquis and Madame de Salres had left, Perry had immediately started to put in hand the desperately needed repairs to the house.

He had summoned, Kezia thought, every workman in the whole district and there was pandemonium taking place around them from dawn until dusk.

There were men on the roof, men repairing the windows and painters and carpenters inside and outside the house.

Perry at the same time began to repair the farm buildings and told Kezia that she was to make a list of what was required for the pensioners' cottages in the village.

This, she reckoned, was one of the most difficult tasks of them all.

The old men and women in the cottages were so excited about what was happening that they wanted to talk.

What was more, she had to find them accommodation while their cottages were in some cases being practically rebuilt.

A week went by in a flash before she realised that she had had no chance to buy any new clothes in London.

Anyway it was quite obvious that, if she wanted to do so, Perry would not have the time to take her to Bond Street.

She was thinking despairingly that she would have to find some time to alter what was hanging in her mother's wardrobe when she came back to the house for luncheon.

She had been in the village all the morning and was still only halfway through her list of what had to be done.

She was late and she hurried the old horse she was riding as quickly as he would go up the drive.

She dismounted at the front door and, taking off his bridle and saddle, left him to find his own way to the stables.

It was something that he had done before and she knew as she had filled his stall with oats early in the morning that he would be eager to get back to it.

Perry was already interviewing grooms and talking of buying horses at Tattersalls, but the necessary repairs had to be completed first.

Kezia walked in through the front door to see to her astonishment that there was a huge pile of boxes on the floor.

When she looked at them closely, she saw they were dress boxes and there were several round ones, which undoubtedly had been made to contain bonnets.

She stared at them and, as she did so, Dennis, a young man they had engaged from the village to help old Humber, came into the hall.

"What are these?" Kezia asked him. "And when did they arrive?"

He was a rather slow-witted youth who found it difficult to answer two questions at once.

After a pause, while he was obviously thinking, he said,

"They comes about 'alf an hour ago, miss, in one of them post chaises."

"A post chaise!" Kezia exclaimed, knowing full well that this type of delivery would be very expensive.

Then, as she bent down to look at what was written on the label of one of the boxes, she read,

"*Madame Marie Bertin, 26 Bond Street.*"

Then Dennis added after a moment's pause,

"There be a letter, miss, and I puts it on the table."

Kezia walked over to the table and picked up the envelope, noting when she opened it that the letter inside contained the words at the top of the page,

"*Madame Marie Bertin.*"

Then she read,

"With the compliments of Madame de Salres to thank you for such a delightful visit."

She studied the handwriting carefully and knew from the way that Madame de Salres had signed the visitors' book that it was not her hand.

Picking up one of the boxes in her arms, she told Dennis to bring the rest of them up to her bedroom.

"Your luncheon be ready, miss," he then stated.

"Bring these up first, please," Kezia replied.

She knew as she spoke that it would be impossible for her to eat without first having her curiosity assuaged.

She put one of the cardboard boxes down on her bed, opened it and then drew in her breath.

Lying inside was the most beautiful evening gown that she could possibly imagine.

When she lifted it out of the box, she found that it had a bertha that was of lace delicately embroidered with tiny *diamanté* like dewdrops and very small pearls.

The skirt that billowed out from a tight-fitting waist was as large, if not larger, than those of the gowns worn by Madame de Salres.

Only when every dress box was unpacked did she find she had been given three evening gowns, three day dresses and what she had wanted herself, a travelling gown. And to wear over it when she crossed the English Channel was a matching cloak.

Every gown to Kezia screamed out the one word, *Paris*.

There was no need for her to be told that Madame Bertin must be a very smart and very very expensive dressmaker to have a shop in Bond Street.

Even before she opened the round boxes to find inside bonnets to match the gowns, she was suspicious.

Yet she knew that there was nothing that she could do about it.

She was absolutely certain that Madame de Salres, who had been polite to her only on the last day of her visit, would not have given her such a magnificent present even if she could afford to do so.

It would be impossible for her to return the gifts or to accuse the Marquis, as she would like to do, of being responsible for them.

If she did so, she was quite certain that he would deny it and only make her look foolish.

Despite the fact that she told herself that she should feel angry, if not insulted, by his behaviour, her heart leapt because he had actually thought of her.

He had been perceptive enough to appreciate that she would be embarrassed to stay with him in France dressed as she had been when he had last seen her.

She wondered if Perry would believe that Madame de Salres was her benefactor.

Then she thought that unless his attention was deliberately drawn to them, he would not even notice the difference in her clothes.

He was totally obsessed at the moment with all the repairs and renovations to the house.

He was so thrilled at being able to afford them that he had even forgotten the necklace and that they had to take it with them to France.

*

Then the day before they were due to leave it arrived, again by post chaise.

With it came a letter from the Marquis's secretary explaining what was arranged for their journey and Perry was surprised.

"Good Heavens!" he then exclaimed. "I had completely forgotten that we are to take the necklace to Bayeux!"

He opened the box to look at it again and suggested,

"I wonder what would happen if we just kept it as well as the money?"

Kezia gave a cry of horror.

"How can you think of anything so crooked?" she asked him.

"I was only joking," Perry replied, "but it must be nice to be as rich as Midas. As far as I can see, he has spent another fortune on the setting."

It was certainly a great improvement as the huge diamonds of the original necklace were now surrounded with smaller ones and the links between them were also diamonds.

"Would you like to try it on?" Perry asked her.

Kezia shook her head.

"No, I think it is unlucky and the best place for it is in the Museum, where it will not make any woman so envious as the Comtesse de la Motte was that she tried to steal it."

"If she received as much money as we did for it," Perry replied, "I rather think it was worth it!"

"You are not to think of such things," Kezia scolded him, "but actually it has been very lucky for us!"

"Very lucky indeed," Perry agreed seriously. "And because of it the Marquis is doing us proud on our journey to Bayeux."

That was indeed an understatement, Kezia thought later, when a smart chaise drawn by six horses arrived to convey them to Southampton.

They spent a night on the way staying with the Marquis's friend, the Duke of Alderstone. He was genuinely pleased to see them and arranged a large dinner party for them to meet his friends.

When they set off again the next morning, Kezia recognised that a crucial part of the enjoyment of the previous evening was that she was so much better dressed than the other ladies present.

For the first time in her life women were looking at her in envy rather than compassion!

The Marquis's yacht was large and very comfortable and it took them only three hours to cross the English Channel.

When she set foot on French soil, Kezia wondered if they were landing at the same place as the Vikings whose invasion had resulted in the Marquis being born with blue eyes.

Perhaps that was also the reason why he was so perceptive. He was so unlike any man she had ever met before and she was sure that it was because he was a Norman.

He came from a race of men who were trained to use their instinct in battle and on the sea, men who were continually fighting against greater forces than themselves.

Conflict had obviously sharpened their wits and maybe at the same time it had developed their inner vision.

They were able to escape death more easily than other men who did not or could not use what the Ancient Egyptians called their *Third Eye*.

When she thought that this was what the Marquis possessed, she gave a little shiver in case he suspected that she had been lying to him.

"Don't forget that I am your wife," she had admonished Perry as they set off from the Port of Southampton in a large and luxurious carriage drawn by four horses.

"I am very glad you reminded me," he said, "and for Heaven's sake, be careful of the Marquis! Do *not* forget what Harry told me about him."

"I-I have not – forgotten," Kezia said in a low voice.

It was something that she thought about very often. In her own way she was being as much of a 'lunatic' as the other foolish women who had lost their hearts to this 'modern Casanova'.

They drove on for a little way and both Kezia and Perry were looking out of the carriage windows at the countryside. It was surprisingly like the one that they had just left on the other side of the English Channel.

Then, for the first time Perry noticed Kezia's bonnet and he remarked,

"You look very smart. Where did you get these clothes? I thought you wanted me to take you into London."

"They *came* from London!" Kezia replied truthfully.

"So you sent for them," Perry said casually. "That was sensible. I could not have found the time to drive you there when there was so much to do at home."

As if the subject no longer interested him, he went on,

"I have just been thinking. If we enlarge the kitchen slightly, it will be much easier for the servants when we give a big party."

Kezia looked at him with frightened eyes.

"A – big party? Oh, Perry, when we have done everything that needs to be done, will we be able to afford it?"

"I am being very careful, I really am," he replied, "but I was thinking that, when the house looks as it should, I would like to invite some of my friends to stay and, if the Marquis can give a Steeplechase, so can I."

"That would be very exciting!" Kezia smiled.

Equally she was thinking that, if they were not careful, in a year or two they would be in the same position as they had been before the Marquis had bought the necklace. And for the next few miles she worried herself over the future.

Then, when she had her first sight of the Marquis's Château, she forgot everything but what was happening to her at that precise moment.

Never in her life had she imagined that anything could be so beautiful and yet so large and imposing.

When they drew a little nearer to the Château itself, she could see that there were five fountains playing in front of the enormous, perfectly proportioned building.

There was a large fountain in the middle and four others in the formal garden that she had read about in books but had never seen before.

Then there were sweeping curved steps leading up to an impressive front door and, as the carriage drew up beside them, the Marquis came out to greet them.

Kezia told herself severely that she must be very controlled and dignified and not let him have the slightest idea what her real feelings for him were.

But, as he raised her hand to his lips and looked at her with his blue eyes, she could only remember how handsome he was.

He also had the same irresistible force that drew her to him like a magnet.

"You have come," he announced in a low voice. "And you are even more beautiful than I remember!"

She wanted to appear indifferent to his compliments.

Instead the colour rose in her cheeks and her eyelashes fluttered because she felt shy and overcome.

Although she was not aware of it, she looked unbelievably lovely in her new gown and the Marquis could not have failed to notice it.

He then led them inside his Château and she could see the painted ceilings, the statues and tapestries and the magnificent array of inlaid French furniture. It was a unique craft that Kezia had read about and had always wanted to see for herself.

It was all very beautiful, but at the same time she was more concerned with the Marquis himself.

She could only listen to his deep voice, which held a note of sincerity that she told herself she had to disbelieve.

But it was impossible for her to think of anything or anyone else.

She was not surprised to find at the Château a large number of the Marquis's relations.

Her mother had told her that the French all gathered round the Head of the Family, who in this case was the Marquis.

Kezia was next introduced to his mother, who was still beautiful, his grandmother and a number of cousins.

There was a very attractive dark-haired girl waiting to be introduced.

"This is Lissette – the Comtesse de Marnay," the Marquis said. "She is my niece and, after she was widowed, she came here to live."

"It is much more exciting here with you, Cousin Vere, than at home," she smiled, "where everybody seems to be over eighty!"

The Marquis laughed.

"What you really mean," he said, "is that we are nearer to Paris than your parents and therefore there are more young men to flatter you!"

"What else are men for?" Lissette grinned.

Perry laughed as the Marquis introduced him.

Kezia was then taken upstairs.

And when she was shown into her bedroom by the housekeeper, she had the idea that the Marquis had deliberately chosen the most magnificent of his State Rooms to show her that, while the rooms at home were impressive, he could do much better.

The ceiling was a riot of cupids chasing after Venus and the bed, with its silk curtains and carved canopy, was like a Papal Throne and the *Aubusson* carpet was brilliant with roses.

Their luggage had been brought from the yacht in a brake and Kezia thought that the only things missing were a valet for Perry and a lady's maid for her.

She was quite certain, however, that the two maids who were unpacking for her would manage her clothes very much better than any village girl and she would have been the only maid she could have provided for herself at such short notice.

Because it had taken them almost a day to reach the yacht, cross the Channel and arrive at the Château, Kezia found that she was expected to rest before dinner and, because she had so much to think about, she was glad to do so.

She did not sleep, but instructed herself sternly to be very careful not to let the Marquis have the slightest suspicion that she was interested in him as a man.

At the same time she wanted to enjoy every moment of her visit to France because this would never happen to her again.

She went down to dinner in one of her new gowns.

The expression in the Marquis's eyes as she entered the room convinced her without any doubt that it was he who had paid for what she was wearing.

'He had no – right to do – such a thing!' she told herself.

But, when she saw the gowns worn by his relatives, she knew how miserable she would have felt if she had come dressed as she had intended.

The gowns that had belonged to her mother were pretty, but completely out of date and she wore tonight the one that she had unpacked first with its beautifully embroidered bertha.

It was white, but not the white that could be very unbecoming even to a *debutante* and the material of the gown had the translucence of a pearl that shimmered in the light of the chandeliers.

The Marquis was looking magnificent in his evening clothes, just as he had when he was staying with them in England.

His relatives were not over-bejewelled as Madame de Salres had been. But Kezia knew that the diamonds, the pearls and the other precious stones they wore in their hair and round their necks were priceless.

What was more they had a family connection in that they had been handed down from generation to generation.

There were twenty people sitting down in the large Banqueting Hall for dinner and the Marquis turned to Kezia as they started the meal,

"As I thought you might be tired, it is just a family occasion tonight."

Kezia laughed.

"You must feel lucky to have such a large family?"

"I am indeed lucky," the Marquis replied, "because I make sure they obey me and do not dare to argue at whatever I wish to do."

"Then, of course, you are extremely spoilt," Kezia teased him, "although undoubtedly any Englishman would think you were very fortunate."

"Are you suggesting that your husband and other men who are married are henpecked by their wives?" the Marquis enquired.

"I was only thinking of the older generation," Kezia replied. "After all I suspect that to your mother and grandmother you will always be a little boy who is getting into mischief!"

"That is something I would like to do if you would help me," the Marquis smiled.

She had the idea as he spoke that it was a remark that he might have made to someone like Madame de Salres with its obvious innuendo.

Instinctively she stiffened.

Because he obviously realised that he had made a mistake, he then started to tell her the history of some of the pictures that covered the walls.

Next he told her of the colourful legends that had grown up around the Château itself.

Because it was so enthralling for Kesia, they were three-quarters of the way through the meal before she realised that she had not talked to the gentleman on her other side.

Apologetically she turned to say to him now,

"Please forgive me if I appear to be neglecting you, but I find the history of this beautiful Château so unbelievably enthralling."

"And doubtless the very eloquent teller of such tales as well!" her neighbour replied.

The way he spoke rather surprised Kezia and, when she looked at him, she thought that there was something that she did not particularly like about him.

"Will you tell me who you are?" she asked. "I find it difficult to remember names the first time I hear them."

"I am Orvil de Bayeux," he replied, "and the 'Black Sheep' of the family!"

Kezia laughed.

"Why should you be that?"

"Because I am invariably in trouble," he admitted, "and therefore I seldom come home unless I cannot help it."

Kezia was surprised at his frankness as he went on,

"At the same time I cannot resist a Steeplechase and, as Vere's horses are much better than anything I can afford, I am prepared to ride the best of them. Also I shall enjoy winning one of the prizes he hands out so generously."

Because he seemed to sneer the last words, Kezia asked him curiously,

"What sort of prizes?"

"If you are thinking of silver pots and all that nonsense, forget it," the Frenchman said. "What I intend to win are the gold Louis that are dished out by Vere to every winner because he can easily afford them!"

Now there was a note of envy and greed in the speaker's voice and Kezia felt rather embarrassed.

As if he realised the effect of his words, Orvil laughed rather unpleasantly.

"I expect, as Guest of Honour, you will help him dispense his family fortune in such an absurd way! While my pockets are empty and I sometimes wonder where my next meal is coming from."

"I cannot believe it," Kezia murmured.

It hurt her to hear the Marquis being disparaged in such a way, but Orvil continued,

"It is true and my only hope is that Vere will continue to remain a bachelor. If he breaks his neck, there is some chance of my inheriting the title and the estate!"

"How can you say such unkind things?" Kezia asked indignantly.

"Are you standing up for him?" Orvil then enquired. "In which case you are obviously besotted by him, like all the other silly women who constantly hover around him like vultures round a carcass!"

Kezia drew in her breath and Orvil carried on mockingly,

"If he fancies you, well, keep him that way. You are married and from my point of view quite harmless!"

He laughed and it was an unpleasant sound.

"It raised my aunt's and my grandmother's hopes for a moment when he came back from England and said that he was inviting a new beauty to stay. They thought it was some nice innocent girl he might take as his wife and for a while I was afraid – "

"How can you talk like that?" Kezia interrupted him.

"But I need not have worried," Orvil ground on. "You are married and just like all the others he will tire of you in time and then he will be looking for another mesmerised little rabbit!"

He sounded so rude that Kezia could hardly believe what she was hearing even though it did sound a little better in French than it would have done in English.

As Orvil finished off his glass of wine, which was continually being refilled by the footmen, she realised that he had had too much to drink.

She knew as she turned back to talk to the Marquis that he had heard what his brother had said to her and she could see the anger in his eyes.

But he only said quietly,

"After dinner I would like to show you some of my pictures."

"I would love to see them and tomorrow, if there is time, I would like to see all over this sublime Château."

"There will always be time for us to do the things we really want to do," he replied.

The ladies and the gentlemen then all left the dining room together as was the custom in France.

When they went back to the salon, Kezia saw that Perry was still talking animatedly with Lissette as he had been at dinner.

As the Marquis joined her, she said, because it was uppermost in her mind,

"How pretty your niece is. It must have been very sad for her to have been widowed so young."

"It would have been indeed," the Marquis agreed, "if she had not after two years been disillusioned by her husband."

"Disillusioned?" Kezia queried.

"He was very rich and very spoilt," the Marquis said, "and he was also half-Greek."

Kezia looked surprised and he explained,

"His mother was Greek and, because he was her only child, she spoilt him abominably with the result that he never considered anybody else but himself."

"So Lissette was unhappy," Kezia said softly.

"Shall I say that she was not at all unhappy when she was freed from what had been an arranged marriage?"

"Now I understand," Kezia responded. "I had forgotten that in France you have arranged marriages and it is something that I think is wrong and can definitely lead to unhappiness and misery."

"That is true," the Marquis agreed quietly.

They walked, as they were talking, towards the end of the room where, hanging on the wall there was a very fine Poussin.

The way he spoke made Kezia think for the first time that perhaps he had been married.

After all she remembered now that every European aristocrat had his marriage arranged for him by his family when he was very young.

She wanted to ask him if this was true in his case, but then felt shyly that it would be an embarrassing question.

As it happened, there was no need for her to ask him for he then said,

"As you are thinking about it, my father arranged my marriage when I was twenty-two."

"And you were unhappy?"

"The Wedding did not take place, I am very thankful to say," the Marquis replied. "My fiancée ran away two weeks before it should have happened."

Kezia gave an exclamation.

"Surely that must have been very upsetting for you? It must have made you feel very unhappy."

"Humiliated, but not unhappy. I had suspected from the first moment that we became officially engaged that she was not really interested in me but in somebody else."

He coughed before he resumed,

"But in those days I was foolish enough to let others manipulate me, which is something that I have never allowed to happen since,"

There was a note of ruthlessness in his voice that Kezia recognised as he went on,

"It was a merciful deliverance and I never gambled with my happiness again, thinking it too great a risk."

Kezia thought of Orvil and how unpleasant he had been and she declared impetuously,

"But, of course, you must marry! You must have a son to inherit this wonderful Château and, while there are many women who love you, there must be someone – you can love!"

They had stopped in front of a picture and, as she looked at it, the Marquis said slowly,

"And suppose I was in love with someone who I could not marry?"

Kezia thought at once of Madame de Salres and doubtless she had a husband somewhere.

For a moment she tried to think of some way that he could marry the woman he loved and be happy.

Then, as she thought of him being married, she was aware that a sharp pain was in her breast and she made herself say lightly,

"I thought you told me that you are a Norman – and therefore a conqueror!"

"Are you really inciting me to take what I want and then damn the consequences?" the Marquis asked.

He spoke in English and, because he sounded so very forceful, Kezia laughed.

"Who could resist you riding down from the North and pointing your lance?"

"I will answer that question another time," the Marquis said unexpectedly. "Now I want you to look at this picture."

With an effort Kezia forced herself to view the Poussin.

Even as she did so, she was aware only of the Marquis's vibrations and the strength of them.

'It is a great mistake for me to be so near to him,' she told herself frantically.

She looked round for Perry, feeling that in some way she should seek his protection.

But he was not with the Marquis's relatives who were sitting at the other end of the *salon*.

There was a window open onto the terrace outside and she knew without being told that Perry and Lissette had gone out into the moonlight.

"Shall we join them?" the Marquis suggested.

"No, of course not!" Kezia said hastily. "I was only looking for Perry because I know how much he would enjoy seeing this beautiful picture."

"I am sure he will enjoy it tomorrow."

Kezia realised then that once again he had been reading her thoughts.

Because she was suddenly frightened that he would know what she felt about him and how, although she could not even explain it to herself, it was like an ecstasy to be near him, she said,

"As it has been a long day and I am tired, will you forgive me if I go upstairs to bed?"

"Yes, of course," the Marquis said, "I want you to feel well tomorrow and I thought if you agree we could go riding before breakfast and before any of my other guests who are taking part in the Steeplechase return to the house."

"I would love that," Kezia replied.

Suddenly she remembered that among the clothes that Madame de Salres had supposedly sent her, there had not been a riding habit.

She hesitated, thinking of the threadbare skirt and darned blouse that she had worn with him at home.

"Will we be riding – alone?" she asked, "because I am – afraid I will not look very – smart."

"I think you will find everything you may require upstairs," the Marquis said, "and I should have told you before now that you look exactly as I want you to."

Kezia looked up at him.

"It was wrong – very wrong of you, but I don't – know what I – can do about it."

"Why should you do anything but look very very lovely?" he asked her.

Because there was no answer to this and she was still afraid of her own feelings, which seemed to flicker through her like little flames of fire, she turned towards the door.

"If I – slip away," she said, "perhaps no one will – notice."

"*I* shall notice," the Marquis asserted. "But tomorrow morning I shall be waiting in the hall for you at seven o'clock."

He opened the door for her and followed her into the hall.

There were four footmen in attendance, resplendent in elaborate gold-bedecked livery.

Kezia stopped at the foot of the stairs.

"Goodnight, *monsieur*," she said softly. "Thank you for a great many things that I must not mention."

"Goodnight, Kezia," the Marquis smiled.

He raised her hand to his lips and once again she felt his mouth against her skin.

Then, as not only her fingers but her whole body quivered with an inexpressible rapture, she ran up the stairs two at a time.

When she reached the landing, she wanted to look back, but thought that the Marquis was watching for her to do so and it would be a mistake.

Therefore, with her face averted, she walked to her bedroom.

Only when she was out of sight did the Marquis slowly and with a strange expression in his blue eyes walk back into the salon.

CHAPTER SIX

Riding over the flat fields beyond the gardens and woods that surrounded the Château, Kezia thought that she had never been so happy.

As she had anticipated when she looked into her wardrobe after having left the Marquis the previous night, she found a riding habit.

It was something else that she knew she should refuse if she was behaving properly as a lady should.

Yet it was impossible not to accept a habit that was different from anything that she had seen anywhere.

It was so French and so *chic* that it made her thrill just to look at it.

Of a deep blue it was frogged with white braid and the lace of the white muslin blouse that went under it was so delicate that she thought it must have been made by the nuns of a French Convent.

She looked at it for a long time before finally she undressed and climbed into bed.

Then, as she went over the conversations that she had had with the Marquis, the rapture she had felt when she had left him downstairs gradually faded.

Of course he was in love with Madame de Salres.

If he could not marry her, then he would remain, as he had done so far, an unusual and perhaps unique French bachelor.

But, as she loved him so much, she tried to understand how, feeling resentful and in a way frightened by the unhappiness he might have experienced in his arranged marriage, he had decided that he would never marry again under any circumstances.

What was unthinkable was to know that his place therefore would eventually be taken by his brother Orvil.

Kezia sensed that he was not only unpleasant but evil.

It was not only what he said or the expression of envy and hatred in his eyes.

It was because she could feel emanating from him something that she could describe only as coming from Satan himself.

Ever since she had come to the Château she had been vividly aware that her perception reacted very strongly to everything in it and that included the people.

She had become even more aware now of the vibrations from the Marquis than she had been when they were in England.

She felt vibrations too from his relatives, especially Orvil and Lissette, and she thought that the young widow was the nicest person in the party with, of course, the exception of the Marquis.

She was glad that Perry could be amused by her rather than by Madame de Salres, whom she was certain was a bad woman.

'Why must I be so positive about these people?' she asked herself indignantly.

She could not deny her own inner feelings, which had guided her all her life, but never so strongly as they were at the moment.

The Château was delightfully enchanted, she was sure of it, but not just the great rooms.

There was the loveliness and colour of the garden with constant shoots of water from the fountains making psychedelic rainbows against the sky.

It was a glory that she felt had perhaps originated with Duke Rollo and descended down the centuries until it reached the Marquis.

'He is a good man – despite his – reputation,' she decided.

She felt herself blush because he had been so generous to her and so understanding as she was quite certain that no other man would have been.

What Englishman would have contrived to provide her with clothes to wear so that she would not feel shabby and inferior with his relatives and friends?

What Englishman would have made their journey to France so comfortable or remember that she would want to ride and, if she was riding, provide a habit for her?

'How can I not – love him?' she asked defiantly.

~139~

She felt that Venus and the cupids on the ceiling were laughing down at her.

When she finally fell asleep, she dreamt of the Marquis.

Although, when she awoke she could not remember anything that had happened in her dream, she felt strongly that he was near her.

His face was so engraved on her mind that she could almost see him.

*

At exactly seven o'clock Kezia ran down the stairs to find the Marquis waiting for her in the hall.

She knew that, in her new habit, which fitted her exactly and accentuated her figure, she appeared very different from the way she had in England.

She saw his eyes flicker over her and she said a little shyly,

"I know it is – incorrect and – perhaps wrong – but there is nothing I can do about it."

"Nothing," he agreed. "And now the horses are waiting."

There seemed to be nobody else in the party to join them and there were only two horses outside with grooms at their heads

The Marquis lifted her gently into the saddle.

Despite her every resolution, Kezia felt herself thrill as his hands touched her and she was close to him.

Then, as she lifted the reins, she tried to think of nothing but the horse she was riding.

They did not speak until they had galloped for quite a long distance and then the Marquis pulled in his stallion and Kezia did the same with hers.

"That was wonderful!" she exclaimed.

Then, as her eyes met the Marquis's, she looked away rapidly and told herself not to be beguiled by anything he said or by the way he was gazing at her.

'He loves Madame de Salres,' she murmured beneath her breath. 'And he compliments every woman he is with, so I would be very foolish to believe him.'

They walked their horses a little way and then the Marquis stopped and turned to Kesia,

"I want you to turn round and look at the Château from here. It is, in my opinion, the best view of my home."

Obediently Kezia turned her horse.

The Marquis was right.

The Château looked so magnificent and at the same time so beautiful that she thought it must be a mirage from another world.

She could see the sun glinting on its many windows and the water from the fountain and beyond there were the tall fir trees.

As she was still drinking in the beauty of the Château, a flight of white doves, which she had noticed before in the garden, flew across the Château.

There were quite a number of them and the Marquis said softly,

"The birds that belong to Aphrodite."

"They are very beautiful like everything else you have surrounded yourself with," Kezia remarked, "so how could you not be happy?"

The Marquis was looking rather wistfully at the Château and after a moment he said,

"I am often lonely in my heart."

He did not have to explain and Kezia knew instinctively exactly what he meant.

He might be surrounded by people, but there was something missing, something spiritual that they could not give him, not even the enchanting ladies who he spent so much of his time with.

Then she asked herself why was that true?

Before she could formulate the question to ask him for an explanation, he went on,

"I think you are aware that, while in our passage through life we encounter love in one form or another, it is rarely the perfection we seek."

He spoke so seriously that Kezia was surprised and she answered,

"I know – very little about love – but I think I understand that perhaps because you are more demanding and so more – discerning than other men – what you are offered is – not enough."

She thought as she spoke of the many women who had laid their hearts at his feet.

They had become, as Harry had said, so obsessed by him that they were 'lunatics' where he was concerned.

And she wondered why he could not love at least one of them as overwhelmingly as they obviously loved him.

"I know what you are thinking," the Marquis said, "but I can swear to you, Kezia, that I have tried to find a woman who not only captures my heart but my soul as well."

"Perhaps – you are asking – too much," Kezia suggested hesitatingly.

"It happens to other men. So why not to me?"

He spoke sharply, almost harshly, and Kezia replied,

"You are still young and you must go on reaching for the stars even though, if you touch them, you might be disappointed."

"I am quite certain that, if I touched the star I am seeking, I would not be disappointed," the Marquis countered firmly. "In fact it would be the miracle that I have been praying for."

It seemed so strange that he should pray as she always had. She prayed every night that one day she would find a man whom she loved beyond peradventure and who loved her in the same way as her father and mother had loved each other.

They had been so happy and so complete in themselves.

"Are you surprised," the Marquis asked in a hard voice that seemed to Kezia somewhat hurtful, "that I should pray?"

"I am just a little – surprised that you – admit to it," Kezia replied. "Most men would be too shy to say so."

"I am not shy and I have prayed that I shall find the love that I seek and it will not be out of reach."

Again it flashed through Kezia's mind that he was thinking of Madame de Salres.

Because she loved him and because she wanted him to have what he wanted in life, she said softly,

"I too will – pray that you will – find what you are – seeking, the miracle will happen and it can be yours."

"Thank you," the Marquis said quietly, "and I have the feeling, Kezia, that your prayer will be heard."

Then, as if there was nothing more to say, he turned his horse.

As Kezia then did the same, they went off at a gallop, jumping several hedges in quick succession.

When they arrived back at the Château, Kezia's cheeks were flushed and her eyes were shining with happiness.

She only wished that she could go on riding with the Marquis forever, perhaps to some distant horizon where the world came to an end and there would be a Heaven which would be theirs for Eternity.

She realised that she was only romancing and there was a great deal for him to do today and she was lucky to have been with him alone for a time.

She ran upstairs to her bedroom to change.

She was just putting on one of her pretty gowns without bothering to ring for the maid when there was a knock on her door and Perry came in.

He was dressed in riding clothes and looked, she thought, particularly handsome and at the same time very English.

"I am just going down to breakfast," he told her, "and then to the stables to choose which horse I shall ride today. The Marquis has told me that I can have any one I want, except for the one he requires himself."

"Oh, Perry, how marvellous!" Kezia exclaimed. "But do hurry in case the Marquis's brother, Orvil, takes the best one before you get there."

"Orvil!" Perry exclaimed. "I think he is an unpleasant chap and the Comtesse told me last night in confidence that he is heartily disliked by the whole family and causes scandal after scandal in Paris."

"It must be very worrying for the Marquis," Kezia murmured.

"I suppose he has to have some problems considering how much he already has and how rich he is," Perry remarked.

There was a note of envy in her brother's voice, which made Kezia say quickly,

"Do not speak like Orvil de Bayeux, who was horrible last night, and anyway had too much to drink."

"Have nothing to do with him," Perry said sharply, "and for Heaven's sake, Kezia, don't fall in love with the Marquis!"

Kezia did not reply to this and he went on,

"Harry warned us what he was like and, although there is no sign of Madame de Salres, I expect either she or another woman like her will be waiting for the Marquis in Paris where he will return as soon as this party is over."

Kezia felt a pain in her breast at the thought of it.

Then in defence of the Marquis she parried,

"You seem quite content to like him at the moment."

As she spoke, she was aware that Perry glanced at her sharply.

"If he is suggesting love to you," he said, "you are not to listen. Do you understand, Kezia? I am certainly not having you breaking your heart over a Frenchman whose reputation is disgraceful from an English point of view!"

Kezia turned towards the dressing table.

"We have delivered the necklace," she murmured, "and I suppose we are going home tomorrow and so I will never see him again."

"And a good thing too!" Perry said. "At the same time I have asked the Comtesse de Marnay to come to stay with us as soon as the house is finished."

"The Comtesse?" Kezia asked.

"Lissette. She tells me that she has never been to England before and I think she would enjoy staying with us."

He went from the room as he spoke and Kezia looked after him in surprise.

Then she told herself that it would be very nice for Perry to have someone like Lissette to stay.

Perhaps it would mean that he would not be quite so anxious to go to London where he gambled with his rich friends.

Also, although he would not talk to her about it, she was sure that he entertained a good few women of whom her mother would not have approved.

Then, as she looked at her reflection in the mirror, she told herself that Perry was right, she must not listen to the Marquis.

If they talked, as they had this morning, in a way that she had not talked to a man before, she would miss him even more despairingly than she would do at present.

'I love – him!' she whispered to herself. 'But it is only because I am a – foolish girl from the – country, who has never seen – a man like him before.'

She had the uncomfortable feeling that it was a delight that she would not know again in which case she would remain an old maid for the rest of her life.

Because the idea was so frightening, she jumped up and ran downstairs to the breakfast room.

The old ladies were obviously having breakfast in their rooms and there was Lissette and one other young woman amongst the men who were seated round the table.

The Marquis was sitting at the head of it and, as he rose to his feet as Kezia entered, he indicated the chair next to his.

There was therefore nothing she could do but sit where he had suggested.

She was offered several dishes and, when she had taken all that she required, the Marquis said,

"I am sure you are hungry, I know I am! You must therefore eat as much as you can, as luncheon will be late."

"The food here is so delicious," Kezia replied, "that I know if I stayed here for long I should grow very fat!"

She ruminated as she was speaking of how little she and the Humbers had to eat before the Marquis had come to stay.

It was only thanks to him that for a little while at any rate she would not be worrying where the next meal was to come from.

"It is something that must not happen again," the Marquis said quietly.

She was aware that once again he knew exactly what she was thinking.

Because it was embarrassing to think that he had provided them with so much, even though he had

~148~

obtained the necklace by doing so, she blushed and looked away from him.

Then, to her consternation, Orvil rose from where he had been sitting to come and sit next to her as he had done last night.

"I hear, Lady Falcon," he began, "that you had Madame de Salres staying with you in your house in England."

"Yes indeed, she came with your brother," Kezia replied.

"I am surprised that a woman of that sort should be acceptable in a respectable English house!"

Kezia did not answer him and Orvil carried on,

"I saw her yesterday and she was very surprised that you had come to France with your husband."

"She was aware that the Marquis had asked us to bring the necklace that he had acquired for his Museum."

Orvil made a sound of disgust.

"His *Museum*!" he exclaimed. "My brother wastes money on buying a lot of nonsensical objects instead of spending the money as he should on his relatives!"

'And on one relative in particular,' Kezia thought to herself, although she knew that it would be an error to say so.

"I am sure that Madame de Salres will be interested to hear," Orvil went on, "that you enjoyed your ride early this morning. She is, of course, extremely jealous where my brother is concerned."

Kezia did not know what to say.

She knew, of course, that he was being deliberately provocative and his insinuations and the sneering way he spoke made her feel very uncomfortable.

She was certain that he would enjoy upsetting Madame de Salres by exaggerating the importance of her riding alone with the Marquis.

Because he hated his brother, he was out to make trouble. She wondered if she should plead with him to do nothing of the sort, but was sure that he would not listen to her.

Instead she continued eating her breakfast, while finding that the food that she had been deprived of for so long now tasted like sawdust.

It was with a great sense of relief when she realised that Orvil, finding that he could not make her reply to his rudeness, had risen to his feet.

"I am going to the stables, Vere," he proclaimed, "in the hope of selecting one of your much-vaunted horses to carry me to victory!"

"The choice is yours," the Marquis nodded. "And, of course, Orvil, I wish you luck."

"You wish me nothing of the sort," Orvil sneered. "But I shall be delighted, as you well know, to take any money I can get out of you!"

He walked from the room after he had spoken. Although the Marquis said nothing, one or two of his guests murmured amongst themselves and Kezia knew that they were shocked and horrified at the way that Orvil de Bayeux was behaving.

She was not surprised as soon as he had gone when Perry also rose.

As he did so, she heard him saying to Lissette,

"You promised to help me choose the best horse in the stables and I cannot manage it without you."

"I will show you the ones that Uncle Vere thinks are the best," Lissette replied.

They left the room together and, as they closed the door behind them, the Marquis said to Kezia,

"I hope you don't mind my niece helping your husband choose a horse."

Kezia smiled.

"It would be wonderful for Perry if he could win one of your races, but even without winning it is a great experience for him to ride horses as fine as yours."

"If I had thought of it I would have organised a ladies' race," the Marquis said, "which you undoubtedly would have won."

Kezia laughed.

"I am quite happy, after riding this morning, to be a spectator and, if I did win, perhaps the other entrants would be jealous and that would be a mistake."

She wondered as she spoke if Madame de Salres was a rider and then thought it unlikely as she had not wished to ride when she was staying with them in England.

The Marquis then rose to his feet.

"Come along," he urged the other gentlemen seated round the table, "I think we ought to go down to the Racecourse, as the riders who have not been staying at the Château should be arriving by now."

He glanced at Kezia and added,

"There will always be a carriage at the front door to convey you or anybody else to the course when they wish to watch the proceedings."

"Thank you," Kezia smiled.

The gentlemen then left the breakfast room and a lady who was a cousin of the Marquis moved up to sit in the chair beside her.

"I have not seen Vere looking so happy or be so enthusiastic about anything for a long time," she commented.

Kezia looked at her in some surprise.

"I should have thought from all I have heard about him that he is a very happy man."

"Not always when he is at home," the cousin remarked, whose name Kezia had learnt was Teresa.

"Why is that?" Kezia asked.

"I think it is because he finds it very lonely being the Head of a large family," Teresa explained. "He continually has them either begging him for money, fighting with each other or pleading with him to marry and have an heir."

"And that makes him unhappy?"

"You too would be unhappy if you had Orvil as a brother," Teresa stressed frankly.

"I-I can see that he is – somewhat of a problem," Kezia agreed.

She spoke hesitantly choosing her words with care.

She knew that it would be a great mistake for her to seem to be too involved with the Marquis's affairs or to criticise one of his family even someone as unpleasant as his brother.

"To tell the truth," Teresa said, "I am very sorry for Cousin Vere and I am not surprised that he spends so much of his time in Paris."

'With Madame de Salres,' Kezia added silently.

She felt again the pain in her breast that was somehow becoming more agonising

*

The races were exciting and Kezia enjoyed every moment of it.

She watched with delight as Perry won a race by a neck from ten other entrants.

Lissette, who was sitting beside Kezia, clapped her hands and jumped up and down with excitement.

"I told him that it was the best horse in the stables," she said, "and he snatched it right from under the nose of Cousin Orvil, who was determined to win this race!"

It was quite obvious that he was furious at not having done so.

As the riders came back from the course, Kezia thought that she had never seen a man look so angry and she only hoped that he would not be disagreeable to Perry.

She could see Perry dismounting his horse and talking to Lissette animatedly about his win.

It had been an important race and, when Kezia heard that the prize was the equivalent in francs of five hundred pounds, she could hardly believe it.

How had they been so lucky as not only to sell the necklace to the Marquis but now for Perry to have won five hundred pounds from him?

She had a feeling that it was too much and they should not take it, but she knew that both men would laugh at her if she said so.

The Steeplechase was to take place after luncheon.

Perry, having won the first race, it was only fair that the winner should be a neighbour, so Orvil was once again disappointed.

When they went back to the Château for luncheon, the Marquis then told the ladies of the house party to distribute themselves amongst the guests who were not staying in the house.

Kezia found herself sitting next to a man who was older than most of the other riders.

She had learnt that when he was young he was one of the most acclaimed horsemen in France.

"Your husband, *madame*, did very well this morning," he smiled.

"I am very honoured to hear you say so," Kezia replied.

The man, whose name was the Comte d' Outeur, then asked her.

"So you have heard of me?"

"Yes, *monsieur*, and I am very impressed."

"I am too old these days to do too much racing," he went on, "but de Bayeux insisted that I should take part in his Steeplechase and it is a great challenge that I will greatly enjoy, although I have no illusions about winning it."

"I have a feeling that the Marquis will easily do so himself," Kezia said.

"I shall be disappointed if he does not," the Comte replied, "and in this neighbourhood it will undoubtedly be a very popular win."

Kezia must have looked surprised for he added,

"I expect you have been told a lot of rubbish about de Bayeux. The trouble with women is that they talk too much. I can assure you that he is an excellent and kindly landlord and in my opinion a credit to Normandy. In fact we are exceedingly proud of him."

Kezia felt her heart warm at such glowing words.

Then, as she looked at the Marquis at the top of the table, she found that he was gazing at her.

She felt at that very moment as if they were united with each other over time and space.

Then one of the ladies beside him attracted his attention and he turned away.

It was then she knew that, despite all the warnings she had been given, he held her heart in his hands completely.

She would never and could never, however long she lived, love anyone else.

As soon as everybody had received their prizes and the guests from outside had returned home, Kezia went slowly upstairs to lie down on her bed.

She was almost asleep when the door opened and Perry came in.

He crossed the room to sit down on the side of the bed facing her.

"I want to talk to you," he began.

"I am so glad you won that big prize, Perry, and you rode quite brilliantly."

"It is all due to Lissette and that is what I want to talk to you about."

"You told me that she wanted to visit England," Kezia mentioned.

There was silence between them.

Then Perry said bluntly,

"I think I have fallen in love!"

Kezia's eyes opened wide and she sat up in the bed.

"Fallen in love? Oh, Perry – is it possible – so quickly?"

Even as she spoke, she at once knew the answer to her question.

Her father and mother had fallen in love with each other the moment they had first met.

She also knew, if she was to be honest, that it was what had happened to her when she met the Marquis.

"I love her!" Perry stated firmly. "And now I am wondering how I can tell her that you and I are not husband and wife but brother and sister."

Kezia gave a little cry.

"Oh, Perry! Do be careful. The Marquis may well be furious if he realises that we have deceived him and I am sure that his mother and grandmother would be greatly shocked!"

"Then what on earth am I to do?" Perry asked.

He stood up from the bed to walk restlessly round the room.

"I had always thought that all the talk about 'love at first sight' was a lot of rubbish, but now I know that it's true! I have not yet said anything really serious to Lissette, but I could swear that she feels the same way as I do."

"Perhaps," Kezia suggested slowly, "you should wait and tell her what you feel about her when she comes to visit us in England?"

"And have her snapped up by some other man because she thinks I am not available?" Perry asked.

"Then what do you intend to do?" Kezia questioned in a frightened voice.

"I shall tell her the truth and swear her to secrecy," Perry replied, "but I thought it only fair to tell you first what I am intending to do."

"Oh, Perry, you must make her promise that she will not tell the Marquis until after we have left tomorrow."

"All right," Perry agreed, "but I have no wish to leave if the Marquis asks me to stay for a little longer."

"I think we should go home," Kezia proposed, "and you know how much there is for you to do."

She could see that her brother was indecisive and added,

"The sooner we can put the house in good order, the sooner Lissette can come to stay."

She saw Perry's eyes brighten and then he said,

"You don't suppose that she will think that we are not as comfortable as they are here in the Château?"

"And never will be, however hard we try," Kezia laughed. "You know, Perry, we cannot possibly compete with the Marquis or the Château."

Perry smiled a little wryly and then he continued,

"You forget that Lissette is French and she told me last night at dinner that she is a very good cook!"

"As long as she has the right ingredients to cook with, you will be in clover!"

She thought as she spoke how hard it had been at times to find anything to eat at home.

It was only after Perry had gone to his own room that she remembered that Lissette was very rich.

She then sent up a little prayer to her mother that, if Perry was in love, he could marry Lissette and they would be very happy together.

She thought that this would solve all his problems.

Then she thought about herself and knew that, when Perry married, it would be a great mistake for her to stay in the house where she had been the Mistress.

Beside which both Perry and Lissette were young and would want to be alone together.

'I shall have to find — somewhere to — go,' she murmured beneath her breath.

She thought of the relation who was going to present her to the Social world and, if she went to London and could not afford the many gowns that would be required for a *debutante*, that would be no solution.

Then she also knew that in leaving the Marquis she would have no more wish to go to balls or for that matter to be a social success.

'Perhaps I could find a small cottage in the village or on the estate,' she told herself.

She felt suddenly as if her whole world had suddenly turned upside down and she was now alone again.

*

The maids came to tell her that it was time to dress for dinner and she wore the second of the beautiful gowns that had come from Bond Street.

It was different from the one that she had worn last night. Of very pale green, almost the colour of her eyes, it was trimmed with a heavy lace bertha and there was lace decorating the full skirt.

It was plain and yet extremely smart and gave her a special grace that made her look as if she had just stepped in from the woods outside the Château.

She had already been told that Frenchmen were interested in women's clothes and had excellent taste and she thought when she looked at herself in the mirror that, if the Marquis had indeed chosen her gowns, that was indeed true.

As they had been such a large party at luncheon, tonight they were only twelve at dinner as several of the relatives had left when the races were over.

"Have you enjoyed yourself today?" the Marquis asked Kezia, who was sitting next to him as she had last night.

"Every moment!" she answered him enthusiastically. "And you organised everything – brilliantly."

"That is the sort of compliment I like to receive," he replied.

He was looking, she thought, even more handsome than usual.

The sun, which had been very strong in the afternoon, had darkened his skin a little and made him look, she thought, even more like a man who had fought a battle in the heat of the day or ridden against his enemy on a fiery steed.

Then she told herself that she must not concentrate on the Marquis.

Yet, knowing that she was to leave tomorrow, she wanted to keep as many memories of him as possible.

It would be all she would have of him, she thought, to sustain her in the future.

To her relief, Orvil was sitting at the other end of the table.

So she did not have to listen to his sneering remarks, but she was aware that, when he looked at his brother, it was with a very unpleasant expression in his eyes.

Perry and Lissette, who were sitting next to each other, seemed to have a great deal to say and for all intents and purposes had forgotten that anybody else existed.

She saw the Marquis's mother look at them once or twice in surprise and she wondered how she could warn Perry to be more discreet.

Then she told herself that whatever happened now, after tonight it was immaterial and tomorrow they would be leaving anyway.

Then perhaps the Marquis would go to Paris to be with Madame de Salres.

'It is – all over,' Kezia told herself. 'And the – sooner I try to forget about him – the better!'

'What are you thinking about?' the Marquis asked unexpectedly.

Kezia told him the truth.

"I was just wondering what time we would have to leave tomorrow and if we shall have the privilege of crossing the Channel again in your yacht."

"It will be waiting for you whenever you are ready to go," he said, "but must you leave me so quickly?"

Kezia felt her heart leap.

Then, before she could answer, he went on,

"There are so many things I want to show you now, the Steeplechase is finished and you have not yet chosen the horse I am going to give you or indeed seen all of the Château."

"I do want to see it all," Kezia replied in a low voice, "but – Perry and I thought you had – asked us for only two nights."

"Then you are mistaken and I will speak to your husband about it after dinner."

As everyone rose and left the dining room, Kezia saw Perry and Lissette slip away while everyone else went into the salon.

She thought it a mistake, but there was nothing she could do.

The Marquis's mother was now pouring out the coffee and she hoped that their absence would not lead to any comment.

She refused the coffee, feeling that it would keep her awake and she had no wish to lie for hours in the darkness thinking of him.

He came to her side to hand her a small glass of liqueur, saying,

"I want you to try this because it is made by the local monks and I think you will enjoy it."

Kezia took a small sip and found that it was sweet and delicious.

"There is another place I thought you might like to visit," he went on. "It is only a small Monastery, but it has been on my land for over three hundred years and the Chapel is very beautiful."

"I would – love to see it," Kezia replied.

"And so you shall, but first you must see the whole Château and there is one picture I particularly want to show you. Shall we go and look at it now?"

Kezia then put down on a small table the glass of liqueur from which she had taken only a few sips.

The Marquis put his empty coffee cup back on the silver tray beside his mother.

As he did so, his brother Orvil did the same thing and for a moment the two brothers were standing side by side.

As Kezia looked at them both, she could not help thinking what a difference there was between them.

'It might almost be a painting,' she thought, 'of Cain and Abel or of Good and Evil.'

Then, as Orvil made some remark to the Marquis, which she was sure was rude, the door suddenly opened and the butler announced,

"Madame de Salres, *monsieur.*"

The Marquis stiffened in astonishment while everybody else's head turned towards the door.

Slowly, dressed flamboyantly in a red gown and glittering with a profusion of diamonds, Madame de Salres stood for a moment in the doorway looking at the assembled guests.

Then slowly she walked down the room towards them, her eyes on the Marquis.

She was carrying a bouquet of white orchids in her hand, which seemed strange.

But Kezia thought she intended to present them to the Marquis's mother as an apology for arriving uninvited.

Then, as she almost reached the Marquis, she stopped and, addressing him in French, she said,

"*Bonsoir, mon cher,* I can readily see that your brother, Orvil, is right and that you have the Englishwoman you neglected me for when we were together in that most uncomfortable of houses."

The way she spoke was, Kezia thought, deliberately insulting and the Marquis took a step forward to say,

"Now, listen to me, Yvonne – "

"I am not listening to you!" Madame de Salres interrupted. "I have come here to inform you, if you don't know it already, that you have broken my heart and, *despite* the lies you told me to keep me from making a scene when we were in England, I know that you have thrown me aside, as you have thrown so many other women before me!"

"I will not listen to this – " the Marquis began.

"You *will* listen," Madame de Salres insisted, her voice rising, "because there is nothing else you can do about it. You will listen to me and I will show you, my most noble Marquis, that you cannot play every woman false and get away with it. In fact I intend to ensure that there will be no more women in your life, now or ever!"

She almost shrieked the last words and, as the Marquis took a step towards her, Madame de Salres pulled her right hand from under her bouquet of white orchids.

In it she held a pistol.

She was pointing it at the Marquis, who stood still staring at her.

"Don't be foolish, Yvonne!" he said very quietly. "If you kill me, you will stand trial for murder!"

"I know that," Madame de Salres replied, but she smiled and somehow it contorted her lips. "I will not kill you, *mon brave*, no! But you will suffer and there will be no more women in your life!"

It was then that Kezia guessed what she was about to do.

Even as Madame de Salres took aim with the pistol, pointing it at the Marquis below his waist, she threw herself against her.

She forced her arm away from the Marquis, but it was, however, too late!

As she did so, Madame pulled the trigger and the explosion seemed to echo deafeningly through the salon.

There was a loud scream from one of the ladies.

Then slowly, very slowly, Orvil de Bayeux fell backwards onto the carpet.

CHAPTER SEVEN

For a moment everyone present seemed turned to stone.

Then the Marquis stretched out his hand to take the smoking pistol from Madame de Salres's .

As he did so, she turned and then, screaming at the top of her voice, ran down the salon towards the door.

Galvanised into action, two of the men in the party bent over Orvil, but Kezia did not see them.

She felt a sudden darkness beginning to envelop her and she put out her hands to hold onto something that was not there.

She would have fallen had not the Marquis thrown the pistol he was holding into a chair and picked her up in his arms.

He did not speak to anybody.

He merely carried her down the room and, as his relatives behind him all started to talk at once, he went out into the hall.

He almost bumped into a *valet de chambre*, who was just about to enter the salon.

"There was a shot, *monsieur*!" he exclaimed.

"Send a groom immediately for the doctor," the Marquis ordered.

He walked on and started to ascend the stairs.

He was halfway up . before Kezia regained consciousness.

She could not for the moment remember what had just happened, but felt as if she was deafened by the noise of the shot that was still echoing loudly in her ears.

Then, as she realised who held her, she stammered in a small hesitating voice,

"She – she – would have – killed you!"

"But you saved me," the Marquis said quietly.

He walked along the corridor, pushed open the door to Kezia's bedroom and, carrying her in, laid her down carefully on the bed.

"Y-you are not – hurt?"

He did not answer her, he only bent over her, looking at her pale face, her frightened eyes and her trembling lips.

Then his mouth came down on hers.

He kissed her very gently, but Kezia felt as if her whole body came alive.

Without meaning to she tried to move closer to him as the Marquis's lips became more possessive and more insistent.

Then, as Kezia felt as if they were surrounded by a dazzling light that was shining in her body and seeping through her breasts up to her lips, the Marquis raised his head.

For a moment his eyes held hers captive.

Incoherently and in a voice that he could hardly hear she asked,

"Sh-she – has not – h-hurt you?"

"But you saved me," the Marquis said again, "and now I must go down to see what is happening."

Kezia's hands moved, but she did not touch him.

"Don't – leave me," she whispered.

"I will come back," he promised, "just rest and try to forget what has happened."

He looked down at her as if he would imprint her beauty on his mind.

Then he went from the room, closing the door quietly behind him.

Kezia closed her eyes.

Could it really have happened?

Had she been in a nightmare when Madame de Salres had tried to injure the Marquis and by the mercy of God she had been able to save him?

Vaguely she remembered that before she had fainted Orvil had moved or had he fallen?

And she wondered if the shot had wounded him.

Then she remembered that Madame de Salres had said that it was Orvil who had told her that she was staying in the Château with the Marquis.

He must have been determined to make trouble for his brother because he hated him so much.

'Please – God – don't let – him hurt the Marquis,' she prayed.

Then it was impossible to think of anything but the wonder of his kiss and the incredible rapture it had given her.

She had never imagined that a kiss would feel so wonderful!

Or that it could evoke an ecstasy that was indescribable and make her feel that she was flying in the sky and all the angels were singing.

"I love – him! *I love – him!*" she shouted out loud as she had a hundred times last night lying in the same bed as she was now.

Then she remembered that she had thought that he loved Madame de Salres.

Although he might feel ashamed and humiliated at the way she had behaved, he could still have an affection for her.

But whatever he may have felt for anybody else, he had kissed her!

Kezia knew that, if she never saw him again after she returned home, he had captured her heart, drawn it from her body and it was no longer her own.

Because the rapture of the Marquis's kiss made it impossible to think of anything else, she lay quietly in bed for a long time.

Then the door opened and the Marquis came back.

Even before she opened her eyes she sensed that he was there.

She could feel a throbbing sensation in her breast and an inexpressible joy ran through her like sunlight.

Then he was sitting facing her and he asked in his deep voice,

"Are you all right?"

Kezia looked up into his blue eyes and reached out her hand.

"What has – happened?" she asked in a whisper.

The Marquis held her hand closely in both of his.

"Although the bullet was meant for me," he said, "because you thrust the pistol aside, it hit my brother Orvil!"

Kezia's fingers tightened on his.

"Is – is he – dead?"

"Not yet," the Marquis replied, "but the wound is very near to his heart and it is unlikely that he will live long."

Kezia felt as if she had stopped breathing.

Then she groaned,

"It was – my fault – "

"But you saved me," the Marquis said quietly. "And, if Yvonne de Salres had killed me, as she might well have done, it would have been a *crime passionnel*, which is permissible in France."

Kezia was looking up at him and now she was frightened, very frightened.

"What I have told my family who fortunately were the only people present," the Marquis said, "is that it was a regrettable accident and they are all agree that Madame de Salres had brought me an ancient pistol from my Museum and she had no idea that it was loaded."

"That – is a – clever – explanation," Kezia murmured.

"Luckily neither Lissette nor your husband was present and everyone who was is very aware that it would be a great mistake for any of us to be involved in a dreadful scandal."

"And if – your brother – dies?" Kezia asked.

"He will linger, I think, for several days. But there will be no need for us to inform the Police and it will just be a 'regrettable accident'."

"I am – so glad," Kezia whispered, "for – your – sake."

She thought as she spoke that anything which harmed or upset the Marquis was wrong.

He was so handsome and so overwhelmingly magnificent that a scandal would be worse for him than for anybody ordinary and of little consequence.

She tried not to think of Yvonne de Salres and her screaming voice as she had run from the salon.

The Marquis read her thoughts.

"Forget her!" he urged. "She was a mistake and I have been punished for making it. I wanted your visit here with me to be as happy and as glorious as you are yourself."

Because of the deep note in his voice, the colour came back to Kezia's face and her eyelashes fluttered because she was now feeling shy.

The Marquis's hand on hers tightened as he said,

"I have something to ask you, Kezia, something that matters to me more than anything else in the world!"

He spoke so seriously that she looked up at him in surprise.

Then he said very quietly,

"I love you! Will you come away with me and I swear to you by everything I hold sacred that the moment your husband divorces you we will be married!"

For a moment Kezia just stared at him, finding it hard to understand the enormity of what he had just asked her.

He was waiting for her answer.

She thought it could not be true that the Marquis de Bayeux, whose title was one of the most prestigious in France, whose family went back many centuries to the great Duke Rollo, was actually prepared to marry a woman who had been divorced.

She knew that no man could make a greater sacrifice for love.

Once again she felt as if he carried her up to the sky and the light that had been there when he kissed her enveloped them both.

Then she drew in a deep breath and said in a voice that was like the song of a bird,

"I love you – I love you so much – that I don't – know how to – tell you that – "

"That is all I need to know," the Marquis interrupted her.

He bent forward and then he was kissing her once more.

Now it was not the gentle kiss that he had given her before, but his lips were possessive and demanding.

Just for a moment, as if he had lost control of himself, he was kissing her as a conqueror.

He was the victor as a man who had fought a desperate battle and had at the last moment turned defeat into victory.

Only when they were both breathless and Kezia felt as if it was impossible to feel such ecstasy and not die of the wonder of it, did he raise his head.

"You are mine!" he asserted fiercely. "*Mine*, as I meant you to be from the first moment I saw you and no one shall ever take you from me!"

Then he was kissing her again and only when it was difficult to breathe did she make a little movement.

He took his lips from hers.

"Do forgive me, my precious," he went on, "but I have been in Hell these last few days, thinking that you were out of reach and I would never be able to make you love me."

"And I was – so afraid that you were – reading my thoughts – and would know – how much – I – love you."

The Marquis's lips found hers again, but after a moment she pushed him a little way from her.

"I-I have – something to – tell you."

"There is no need for words," the Marquis said. "All we have to decide, you and I, is how soon we can go away together and leave all the explanations and recriminations to take place after we have gone, when we will not be around to hear them."

Kezia recognised that he was thinking of Perry.

Because it was so wonderful that there would be no recriminations, she could not think of the words to tell the Marquis that there was no need for them to disappear.

"What I have planned," he was saying, "is that we will take my yacht and seek, my darling, the first horizon you told me you wished to find. Then travel to the horizon beyond it and the others beyond that!"

Kezia opened her lips to speak, but he went on,

"I have so much to give you and so much to teach you, especially about love."

He bent nearer to her as he asked,

"How can you be so innocent and unspoilt? If I did not know you were married, I would swear you have never been kissed until I kissed you after you had saved me from the bullet that would have crippled me."

"You – are quite – right," Kezia whispered, "I never – have – been kissed."

The Marquis was still.

"What do you mean? I don't understand."

"I-I never – have been – kissed by anyone – but you!"

"That is – impossible!"

In a very small voice Kezia murmured,

"Perhaps – you will be – angry when you – hear the – truth."

"The truth?" the Marquis questioned.

"P-Perry – is my – brother!"

As she spoke, Kezia felt a sudden terror in case, because they had been so deceitful, the Marquis would be shocked and stop loving her.

For a second she could not look at him.

"Your *brother*!" he cried.

Because she was frightened she looked up at him pleadingly.

"F-forgive me – please – forgive me, but Perry thought that it would be a – good idea because his – friend in London had told him – a lot of – lies about your – behaviour with women."

"I am sure they are not lies," the Marquis answered. "But when I saw you I knew that you were the one woman I had been seeking all my life and thought I would never find."

"Did you – really think – that?"

"You are the most beautiful woman I have ever seen," the Marquis answered, "but there is so much more that at first it was impossible for me to believe that you were real."

"I – I am very – real."

"I know that now, but I knew, when you could read my thoughts and I could read yours, that you were different from anyone I have ever encountered and I knew too that I had to make you mine or else lose

~176~

something so incredibly precious that without it I could never be a complete person."

"I-I thought – the same," Kezia whispered, "but I thought – you loved – Madame de Salres."

"I have never loved anyone in the real meaning of the word," the Marquis said firmly, "and it is going to take me a lifetime to explain to you how different what I feel for you is from anything I have ever felt before for anyone."

He drew a deep breath as if a burden had fallen from his shoulders before he said,

"How soon can we be married – tonight, tomorrow?"

Kezia gave a little cry.

"You are going so quickly – I want to be your wife – but only if you are quite – certain that you will not become – bored or disenchanted with me."

"Bored or disenchanted?" the Marquis exclaimed. "Do you really think that is possible?"

There was a note in his voice that made her heart leap.

At the same time she wanted to make absolutely sure that he was not making a mistake.

"You – realise," she said, "how – unsophisticated I am and also – because I am English – I cannot be fascinating and amusing like – Madame de Salres."

The Marquis put his fingers under her chin and turned her face up to his.

"Listen, my darling one, do you really think that I want my wife, and please God the mother of my children, to be like a woman you should never have met, except that I thought your brother was a bachelor?"

He was speaking very seriously and then quite unexpectedly he laughed.

"How can you have deceived me when I pride myself on being perceptive and certainly have had enough experience to have known from the very beginning that you were not a married woman?"

"I was wearing – one of – Mama's gowns," Kezia pointed out.

The Marquis smiled very tenderly.

"It was not what you were wearing, my precious," he said, "but was, I think, because I was so bemused by your beauty and by the vibrations that joined us from the first moment we met, that I found it impossible to think clearly."

He touched the softness of her cheek before he went on,

"All I knew was that my heart and soul told me that I had found what I had been seeking all my life, while my brain then warned me that in my position I must not be involved in a scandal."

"I think," Kezia said, "Perry expected – you to want to make – love to me, but thought it more – difficult if you were – staying in his house and I was his wife."

The Marquis thought privately that Perry had attempted to make him believe that he was guarding his 'wife' not only in the daytime but also at night.

He had, however, no intention of saying anything like that to Kezia.

It was her innocence and purity that had captured him in the first place and he knew that it was something so unique and so different from all the other women he had been interested in.

He vowed silently that he would keep her safe from being soiled by anything ugly or unpleasant in the Social world.

She fitted perfectly into the Château, where he had never brought women like Madame de Salres.

He had kept them in Paris or sometimes taken them to the house of his friends who were less fastidious about their homes than he was.

He had intended, in all sincerity, to leave Kezia, because she was perfect, as she was.

He was determined not to kiss her or try to make love to her, as he had done so many times before with so many women.

Then, when she had saved him from being crippled in a way that would have made him want to take his own life, he lost what had been an iron self-control.

He kissed her because he could not help it.

It was then he knew that without Kesia he had no wish to go on living.

Whatever the scandal, whatever the horror and distress to his mother and his relations, he could not lose her.

Even if it meant that he could no longer return to France, he knew that he could not give up Kezia and all that she meant to him.

Now incredibly the miracle that he had prayed so diligently for had happened.

She was *free*. And he could marry her.

He just knew, with the inner perception that had been his all his life, that they would be unbelievably happy together for the rest of their lives.

The enormity of it made him just sit gazing at her until she asked him a little anxiously,

"Have I – said something – wrong?"

"I have just decided," the Marquis told her quietly, "that we shall be married this evening in the Château Chapel."

"This – evening?"

"I will send my secretary at once to the Maire to register our marriage as is compulsory in France."

Kezia was staring at the Marquis wide-eyed as he added,

"It will be the sensible thing to do. When Orvil dies, there will be a large family funeral, but, if you and I are on our honeymoon, it will be impossible for us to be present."

Then Kezia's quick brain made her understand exactly what he was telling her and she reached out her hands to him saying,

"I will do – whatever you – tell me to – do!"

*

Kezia was in the boudoir that adjoined her bedroom when Perry came in.

Because the maids were busy packing her clothes in her bedroom and at the same time bringing in her bath, she had undressed and put on her *négligée*.

She was standing at the window gazing out at the sky.

The sun was sinking and she sent up a prayer of thankfulness to God because she was so happy.

She was also profusely thanking her father and mother.

'Thank you – *thank you*!' she was saying. 'You have brought me the man I prayed for – and I know it was due to – you both because you were – helping and guiding me.'

"What is going on?" Perry asked as he came into the room. "There is no one downstairs, but the servants tell me that there has been an accident to Orvil."

Kezia walked across the room to him.

"Where have you been?"

Perry smiled.

"I have been in the woods with Lissette," he answered, "and you must congratulate me, Kezia, for I am the happiest man in the world."

"As I am the happiest woman!"

He looked at her in surprise and she explained,

"I am being married – this evening to – the Marquis!"

Perry just stared at her and then he asked,

"Is this a joke?"

"No, of course not," Kezia replied. "I am telling you the truth. As you have heard, the Marquis's brother has had an unfortunate accident and we want to get away in case he dies."

For a moment Perry was silent.

Then he said,

"If he is likely to die, knowing what the French are like when it comes to funerals and mourning, the sooner Lissette and I leave for England the better."

"And – you will be married there?"

"Or here," Perry said, "it does not matter, as long as we don't have to wait very long and she is afraid that her cousin and, of course, his mother might raise objections and say that we should have at least a two or three month engagement."

Kezia laughed.

"The Marquis can hardly insist on that – when he is marrying me so quickly."

"No, of course not," Perry agreed, "and, Kezia, I am really glad about it, if you are really certain that you know how to hold him."

Kezia knew exactly what he was implying and she replied simply,

"Vere tells me that he has been looking for me all his life. I believe him and there is no need for me to – tell you that he is truly the – man of my dreams."

"I knew that you would fall in love with him!" Perry exclaimed.

"And you were quite right," his sister reacted. "He is – irresistible!"

"And that is what I have to be to Lissette. Oh, Kezia, she is so adorable and she says that she will love helping me to do up the house and she does not mind being uncomfortable until we can make it perfect!"

Kezia gave a little laugh.

"Then she is exactly the right wife for you and actually I thought with the exception of the Marquis she was the nicest person in the whole party!"

"We are going to have as good if not better horses than he has," Perry boasted, "and, when you come to stay with us, you can compare them."

"We most certainly will," Kezia promised.

"I had better go now to have my bath," Perry said, walking towards the door.

Only as he reached it did he turn back to ask Kesia as an afterthought,

"By the way I never enquired what has happened to Orvil. What sort of accident did he have?"

"A pistol – was fired and – by mistake, the bullet hit – him," Kezia replied truthfully.

"Oh, is that all?" Perry said and went out of the room, closing the door behind him.

*

It was very quiet in the ancient Chapel when Kezia entered it on Perry's arm.

She saw that the Marquis waiting for her at the Altar.

The only other person present was Lissette, whom Perry had insisted should witness the marriage.

The Marquis had told Kezia just before she went down to dinner that he had decided that they should be married as soon as the rest of the party had retired.

"They will not want to stay up late after what has happened today," he said, "and I hear that my mother and grandmother will not be coming down to dinner."

"Then we shall just be alone – with God," Kezia declared simply.

The Marquis put his arms round her and drew her close to him.

"That is just what I want us to be and, my darling, when I told your brother what I had arranged, he wanted Lissette to be there, as they have decided to be married early tomorrow morning before they leave for England."

Kezia gave a little cry of delight.

"I am so glad. I am sure that Lissette will look after Perry beautifully and make him very happy."

"I have never known a man so excited, except myself," the Marquis smiled, "and I have given my Blessing to the marriage, which will be nearly as wonderful as ours."

"And ours will be – very – very marvellous!" Kezia said in a soft voice.

He kissed her gently.

Then he left the boudoir so that they would not be seen coming down the stairs together, which might cause comment amongst the servants.

*

There were eight people at dinner and the only other woman besides Kezia and Lissette was Teresa.

She, however, complained of a headache and retired to bed after they had drunk their coffee in the salon.

The men then went off to play billiards and the two couples who wished to be married were left alone.

The Marquis smiled.

"What are we waiting for?"

He looked at Kezia and suggested,

"Go and get ready, my darling. My valet will be coming with us on our honeymoon and is the only person in the house who knows what is taking place. He will bring you a veil that has been in my family for at least two hundred years."

Kezia hurried up the stairs.

She was thinking as she did so how fortunate she was that the gown she was wearing, and which the Marquis admitted he had chosen for her, was very suitable for a bride.

It was the same one that she had worn on the first night with the beautifully embroidered bertha.

The shimmering satin was exactly the same colour as the exquisite lace veil, which had yellowed slightly with age. She put it over her hair and held it in place with a magnificent diamond tiara that the Marquis had also sent her.

It had been made by a superlative craftsman of jewellery during the reign of Louis XIV and was fashioned of flowers, which made it, Kezia thought, very suitable for the Château.

She had never worn a tiara before and, when she gazed at herself in the mirror, she knew that it was all part of being in the Fairytale that had been hers ever since she had crossed the English Channel in the Marquis's glorious yacht.

When she had her first sight of the sublime Château with its five fountains throwing their glittering water towards the sky, she thought that she was dreaming.

As soon as she was ready, Perry was waiting to escort her from her room down a side staircase, so that she would not be seen by the servants in the hall.

When they reached the long corridor that led to the Chapel that was at the back of the Château, there was a bouquet of lilies-of-the-valley waiting for her on a chair.

She reckoned that the Marquis had chosen it for her because her room at home was the Lily-of-the-Valley Room.

She thought that only he, with his perceptive mind and fine attention to detail, could have remembered such a loving detail. And only his brilliant organisation would have produced it at the right moment.

She was not surprised to find that in the few hours that had elapsed since he had decided that they should be married this evening, the Chapel had been decorated with white flowers.

With a large number of candles lighting the Altar, it was as beautiful and spellbinding as everything else that belonged to the Marquis.

Since dinner he had added his decorations to his evening coat. He wore a ribbon across his shoulder and a diamond cross beneath his white tie.

Now the organ was playing very softly.

As the Marriage Service proceeded and the Marquis placed a gold ring on Kezia's finger, she knew that the angels and archangels were singing above them.

The music they heard came from their hearts and the song was part of themselves and the light that throbbed within them.

When the Chaplain blessed them, she knew that she had been blessed already in finding love when she had thought it impossible for her.

Because they were so attuned to each other, she knew that the Marquis was thinking the same and thanking God that his search was now over.

When finally they rose from their knees, the Marquis took Kezia down the short aisle and out of the Chapel.

They went up the staircase that she had just descended.

There was no one to see them go, not into her room, but into the Marquis's.

It was even more magnificent than she had anticipated.

But she had eyes only for her husband, who for the moment did not touch her, but only stood looking at her.

"You are mine, my glorious Kezia!" he breathed at last. "Mine from now until Eternity!"

Instinctively Kezia moved closer to him, but he did not kiss her.

Instead he took the tiara from her head and then surprisingly he took a step backwards to look at her.

"Now you are like a Saint and, my darling, I am ready to kneel at your feet and worship you!"

"I would – rather be in – your arms," Kezia whispered.

He pulled her against him and asked,

"How could I have imagined that I should find you when I had decided that because you did not exist I would never marry?"

"And I – thought," Kezia said, "that because we were so – poor and I never saw any – men except for Perry – I should never have the chance of – falling in love!"

"And now the miracle has happened," the Marquis sighed, "and we are together."

He spoke so seriously that Kezia thought that the vows he had made in the Chapel were still in his mind.

Then, as if he was suddenly conscious of his Norman blood, he pulled Kezia close to him and kissed her demandingly.

Once again she was floating in the clouds at the sheer wonder of it.

Her whole body was so completely merged with his that she was hardly aware when he removed her veil, then her gown and dropped them onto the floor.

Only when he lifted her up in his arms did she give a little murmur because she was shy and hid her face against his shoulder.

He set her down against the pillows in the enormous carved bed with its crimson curtains and gilded pillars.

It was very large and, as she looked up at the canopy overhead and beyond it to the exquisitely painted ceiling, she felt rather small and lost.

A second later the Marquis joined her.

He pulled her closely into his arms and she knew then that this was the dream that she had always wanted to dream.

She was safe and enveloped in the love that joined her heart to his heart, her mind to his mind and her body to his body.

"I love you – I *love you*!" she whispered. "Oh, darling, wonderful Vere – I love you with – all of – me!"

"I adore and worship you," he replied, "and, Heart of my Heart, it is something vital that we will never lose for our love as it will grow greater year by year. When we die, we will be together and nothing, not even death, can ever separate us."

Kezia knew that the way he spoke came from his soul. He felt her body quiver against his and realised that he had found the perfection that all men seek in life, but are so often disappointed.

Then he was kissing her, kissing her until they were flying again in the sky.

The heat of the sun was burning in them both and the Divine Light covered them as if the stars had all fallen down.

*

A long time after, when the candles in the gold chandeliers beside the bed were guttering low, Kezia moved against the Marquis's shoulder.

"Are you awake, my precious?" he asked.

"I am too – happy to – sleep," she answered. "I-I did not realise that – love was so – wonderful – so different from anything I could ever have expected."

"What did you expect?" the Marquis wanted to know.

"Something – soft and gentle – like the music of the bees and scent of flowers."

The Marquis pulled her a little closer.

"And what is it like now?"

"It is so – fierce – demanding – and it is – impossible not to be – conquered by it," she whispered.

"I have not frightened or hurt you?"

"No – of course not, but I did not expect making love to be – quite so – overwhelming or so – utterly and completely – wonderful!"

"This is only the beginning," the Marquis promised. "I have so much to teach you and so much to learn myself."

"What can – I teach – you?"

"You can teach me about beauty and, as you are the most beautiful woman I have ever seen, it should not be too difficult. You can teach me to understand people as you do, to be compassionate and to be concerned with their difficulties and problems, as I have tried to be in the past."

His lips were against her cheek as he finished,

"But it was difficult with no one beside me to help and guide me, as I know you will do in the future."

Kezia felt the tears come into her eyes.

"How can you say – anything so – marvellous to – me?" she asked. "It makes me feel – very humble and after all – as you well know – I am very inexperienced – and perhaps rather foolish."

"You are very wise, my magical wife, in the things that really matter, the things that I have been looking for, but alone."

Kezia put her arm protectively across his chest and said,

"Now I know why, although you are strong and omnipotent, I want to – protect you. I want to prevent anything from – hurting you either physically or spiritually. At the same time – I feel safe because you will – look after me."

The Marquis gave a deep sigh.

"How is it possible," he asked, "that after all the sins I have committed, and there have been a number of them, God sent me anyone as sublime as you?"

He kissed her forehead tenderly before he went on,

"Like the Star of Bethlehem I shall follow you in the future in so many ways and yet, as you said, I will look after you and protect you and, if any man comes near you or tries to take you from me, I swear I will kill him!"

He spoke so fiercely that Kezia laughed.

"There speaks the Norman! But you are quite safe, my darling, there is – no man in the – whole world who could look like you – speak like you – or feel like you."

"That is what I want to believe."

He turned towards her, leaning on his elbow.

She thought that he would kiss her, but for the moment he just gazed down at her.

"Tomorrow," he said, "we are leaving on a voyage of discovery to find our real selves, which we have always been hidden from the world because they were too intimate and far too precious."

Kezia was listening attentively as he went on,

"But now we are joined together we will make one complete person and that is what, my lovely, perfect little wife, we are going to be – one complete person."

His hand touched her breast and he went on,

"An example to all those who have sought, as we have, for the love that is different and the love that when one finds it is perfect."

His lips sought Kezia's.

When she could speak again, she said,

"Do you realise, my darling, that all this has – happened because you – wanted to buy a necklace that caused a – great deal of unhappiness – not only for the people involved with it – but to France?"

"A necklace I will never allow you to wear," the Marquis replied, "but I will, however, always treasure it, because it brought me to you."

Then he said,

"But I will buy you a necklace of diamonds and of several other stones to express my love for you with."

Kezia laughed and it was a very happy sound.

"I would much – rather have a necklace of – your kisses and that will be – a present for which I will be – greedy enough to want not once – but many times!"

"It is a present you shall have," the Marquis answered.

He kissed her forehead, her eyes, her little straight nose, but, when her lips were waiting for his, he bent and kissed her neck.

She did not realise in her innocence that this would awake in her different feelings from those she had ever felt before.

As his lips journeyed lovingly over the softness of her skin, she felt a flame like the burning heat of the sun moving through her body into her breasts and up to her lips.

Her breath came quickly between her lips and she stirred beneath him.

"Does that excite my darling?" he asked her.

"It makes – me feel – strange."

"In what way?"

"Very – very – thrilled and – "

Her voice died away.

"And – ?"

"Perhaps you will – be – shocked!"

"Tell me."

"I feel – wild – almost madly excited – can that be – wrong?"

"Wrong! My precious, my adorable, perfect, innocent little wife, it is right and what I want you to feel. This is *Love*, my darling – real Love."

"Oh – Vere!"

It was a cry of inexpressible joy.

Then, as the Marquis completed the circle at the base of her throat, she quivered with a Divine ecstasy that swept through her whole body.

Until, as he made her indivisibly his, there was the music of angels, the light of God and then they were one being.

Complete and perfect in the love that was beauty itself and was theirs for Eternity and beyond.

OTHER BOOKS IN THIS SERIES

The Barbara Cartland Eternal Collection is the unique opportunity to collect all five hundred of the timeless beautiful romantic novels written by the world's most celebrated and enduring romantic author.

Named the Eternal Collection because Barbara's inspiring stories of pure love, just the same as love itself, the books will be published on the internet at the rate of four titles per month until all five hundred are available.

The Eternal Collection, classic pure romance available worldwide for all time.

Made in the USA
Monee, IL
01 August 2021

74695870R00121